I—I Had Seen
Frankenstein's Monster!

There was no mistaking it.

Of its face I had no clear idea.
The twenty-first century 4-D
representations had prepared me for
something horrific, but my impression
was of features far more frightening.

There was another streak of lightning
overhead. Victor Frankenstein had
slumped back against a tree trunk for
support, his head lolling back as if he
were about to collapse in a faint. His
monster, the creature he had created,
was striding toward him. Then blackness
again.

Then more lightning. The gigantic figure
had passed by its creator as if he did
not exist. I saw that its arms did not
swing properly as it walked—but, oh, how
fast it walked!

And then I saw that it was walking
toward me . . .

FRANKENSTEIN
unbound
BY BRIAN ALDISS

WARNER BOOKS

A Warner Communications Company

*My thanks go to M. Jean Neuprez of Geneva
for topographical and historical assistance.
B.W.A.*

WARNER BOOKS EDITION

This Warner Books Edition is published by arrangement with
the author.

Warner Books, Inc.
666 Fifth Avenue
New York, NY 10103

A Warner Communications Company

Printed in the United States of America
First Warner Books Printing: May, 1990

10 9 8 7 6 5 4 3 2 1

For Bob and Kathy Morsberger who
appreciate what Mary Shelley started

Alas, lost mortal! What with guests like these
Hast thou to do? I tremble for thy sake:
Why doth he gaze on thee, and thou on him?
Ah, he unveils his aspect: on his brow
The thunder-scars are graven: from his eye
Glares forth the immortality of hell . . .

Byron: *Manfred*

Make the beaten and conquered pallid, with brows raised and knit together, and let the skin above the brows be all full of lines of pain; at the sides of the nose show the furrows going in an arch from the nostrils and ending where the eye begins, and show the dilation of the nostrils which is the cause of these lines; and let the teeth be parted after the manner of such as cry in lamentation.

Leonardo da Vinci: *Treatise on Painting*

Part one

I

Letter from Joseph Bodenland to his Wife, Mina:

August 20th, 2020   *New Houston*

My dearest Mina,
I will entrust this to good old mail services, since I learn that
CompC, being much more sophisticated, has been entirely dis-
organized by the recent impact-raids. What has not? The head-
line on today's Still is: SPACE/TIME RUPTURED, SCIENTISTS SAY.
Let us only hope the crisis will lead to an immediate conclusion of the war, or who knows where we shall all be in six
months' time!

But to more cheerful things. Routine has now become re-
established in the house, although we still all miss you sorely
(and I most sorely of all). In the silence of the empty rooms at
evening, I hear your footfall. But the grandchildren keep the
least corner occupied during the day. Nurse Gregory is very
good with them.

They were so interesting this morning when they had no
idea I was watching. One advantage about being a deposed
presidential advisor is that all the former spy-devices may now
be used simply for pleasure. I have to admit I am becoming
quite a voyeur in my old age; I study the children intensely. It
seems to me that, in this world of madness, theirs is the only
significant activity.

Neither Tony nor Poll have mentioned their parents since
poor Molly and Dick were killed; perhaps their sense of loss is
too deep, though there is no sign of that in their play. Who
knows? What adult can understand what goes on in a child's
mind? This morning, I suppose, there was some morbidity. But
the game was inspired by a slightly older girl, Doreen, who

came round here to play. You don't know Doreen. Her family are refugees, very nice people from the little I have seen of them, who have arrived in Houston since you left for Indonesia.

Doreen came round on her scouter, which she is just about old enough to drive, and the three of them went to the swimming pool area. It was a glorious morning, and they were all in their swimsuits.

Even little Poll can swim now. As you predicted, the dolphin has been a great help, and both Poll and Tony adore her. They call her Smiley.

The children had a swim with Smiley. I watched for a while and then struggled with my memoirs. But I was too anxious to concentrate; Sec. of State Dean Reede is coming to see me this afternoon and frankly I am not looking forward to the meeting. Old enemies are still old enemies, even when one is out of office – and I no longer derive pleasure from being polite!

When I looked in on the children again, they were very busy. They had moved to the sand area – what they call the Beach. You can picture it: the grey stone wall cutting the leisure area off from the ranch is now almost hidden by tall hollyhocks in full bloom. Outside the changing huts are salvia beds, while the jasmines along the colonnade are all in flower and very fragrant, as well as noisy with bees. It is a perfect spot for children in a dreadful time like the present.

The kids were burying Doreen's scouter! They had their spades and pails out, and were working away with the sand, making a mound over the machine. They were much absorbed. No one seemed to be directing operations. They were working in unison. Only Poll was chattering as usual.

The machine was eventually entirely buried, and they walked solemnly round it to make sure the last gleaming part was covered. After only the briefest discussion, they dashed away to different parts of the area to gather things. I saw their quick brown bodies multiplied on the various screens as I called more and more cameras into action. It looked as if the whole world was tenanted by little lissom savages – an entirely charming illusion!

They came back to the grave time and time again. Sometimes they brought twigs and small branches snapped off the shelter-

8

ing acacias, more often flower-heads. They called to each other as they ran.

Nurse Gregory had the morning off, so they were playing entirely alone.

You may recall that the cameras and microphones are concealed mainly in the pillars of the colonnade. I was not picking up what the children were saying very well because of the constant buzzing of bees in the jasmine – how many secrets of state were saved by those same insects?! But Doreen was talking about a Feast. What they were doing, she insisted, was a Feast. The others did not question what she said. Rather, they echoed it in excitement.

'We'll load on lots of flowers and then it will be a huge, huge Feast,' I heard Poll say.

I gave up work and sat watching them. I tell you, theirs seemed the only meaningful activity in the crazy warring world. And it was inscrutable to me.

Eventually, they had the grave covered with flowers. Several branches of acacia were embedded on top of the mound, which was otherwise studded with big hollyhock flowers, crimson, mauve, maroon, yellow, orange, with an odd scarlet head of salvia here and there, and a bunch of blue cornflowers that Poll picked. Then round the grave they arranged smaller twigs.

The whole thing was done informally, of course. It looked beautiful.

Doreen got down on her knees and began to pray. She made our two solemn grandchildren do likewise.

'God bless you, Jesus, on this bright day!' she said. 'Make this a good Feast, in Thy name!'

Much else she said which I could not hear. The bees were trying to pollinate the microphones, I do believe. But chiefly they were chanting, 'Make this a good Feast, in Thy name!' Then they did a sort of hopping dance about the pretty grave.

You must wonder about this unexpected outbreak of Christianity in our agnostic household. I must say that at first it caused me some regret that I have for so long stifled my own religious feelings in deference to the rationalism of our times – and perhaps partly in deference to you, whose innocent pagan outlook I always admired and hopelessly aspired to. As far as I know, Molly and Dick never taught their children a word of

9

prayer. Perhaps the traditional comforts of religion were exactly what these orphans needed. What if those comforts are illusions? Even the scientists are saying that the fabric of space/time has been ruptured and reality – whatever that may be – is breaking down.

I need not have worried overmuch. The Feast ceremony was basically pagan, the Christian formulae mere frills. For the dance the children did among their plucked flowers was, I'm sure, an instinctual celebration of their own physical health. Round and round the grave they went! Then the dance broke up in rather desultory fashion, and Tony popped his penis out of his trunks and showed it to Doreen. She made some comment, smiling, and that was that. They all ran and jumped into the pool again.

When the gong sounded for lunch and we all assembled on the verandah, Poll insisted on taking me to look at the grave.

'Grampy, come and see our Feast!'

They live in myth. Under the onslaught of school, intellect will break in – crude robber intellect – and myth will wither and die like the bright flowers on their mysterious grave.

And yet that isn't true. Isn't the great overshadowing belief of our time – that ever-increasing production and industrialization bring the greatest happiness for the greatest number all round the globe – a myth to which most people subscribe? But that's a myth of Intellect, not of Being, if such distinction is permissible.

I'm philosophizing again. One of the reasons they chucked me out of the government!

Dean Reede arrives soon. My just deserts, some would say . . .

Write soon.

Ever your loving husband, JOE

PS. I enclose a still of the leader in today's London *Times*. Despite the measured caution of its tone, there's much in what it says.

2

The Times First Leader, August 20th, 2020:

DEADLY RELATIONSHIPS

Western scientists are now in general although not entire accord – for even in the domain of science opinion is rarely unanimous – that mankind is confronted with the gravest crisis of its existence, a crisis not to survive which is not to survive at all.

Crises which in prospect appear uniquely ominous have a habit of assuming family resemblances in retrospect. We observe that they were critical but not conclusive. To say this is not to be facetious. Professor James Ransome's comment in San Francisco yesterday brought a sense of proportion to the increasingly alarmist news of the instability of the infrastructure of space – a sense of proportion particularly welcome to that large general public unaware until a fortnight ago that there was such a thing as an infrastructure of space, let alone that nuclear activity might have rendered it unstable. The professor's remark that the present instability represents, in his words, 'the great grey ultimate in pollution' should remind us that the world has survived serious pollution scares for over fifty years.

However, there are sound reasons for regarding our present crisis as nothing less than unique. All three opposed sides in the war, Western, South American and Third World Powers, have been using nuclear weapons of increasing calibre within the orbits of the Earth-Luna system. Nobody has gained anything, unless one includes the doubtful benefit of having destroyed the civilian Moon colonies, but the general feeling has been one of relief that these weapons were used above rather than below the stratosphere.

Such relief, we now see, was premature. We are learning yet another bitter lesson on the indivisibility of Nature. We have long understood that sea and land formed an interrelated unit. Now – far too late, according to Professor Ransome and his associates – we perceive a hitherto undiscerned relationship between our planet and the infrastructure of space which surrounds and supports it. The infrastructure has been destroyed, or at least damaged, to the point at which it malfunctions unpredictably, and we are now faced with the consequences. Both time and space have gone 'on the blink', as the saying has it. We can no longer rely even on the sane sequence of temporal progression; tomorrow may prove to be last week, or last century, or the Age of the Pharaohs. The Intellect has made our planet unsafe for intellect. We are suffering from the curse that was Baron Frankenstein's in Mary Shelley's novel: by seeking to control too much, we have lost control of ourselves.

Before we go down in madness, the most terrible war in history, largely an irrational war of varying skin-tones, must be brought to an immediate halt. If the plateau of civilization, on to which mankind climbed with such long exertion, now has to be evacuated, let us at least head away into the darkness in good order. We should be able to perceive at last (and that phase 'at last' now contains grim overtones) that, as the relationship between space, planets, and time is more intimate and intricate than we had carelessly imagined, so too may be the relationship between black, white, yellow, red, and all the flesh-tones in between.

3

Letter from Joseph Bodenland to his Wife, Mina:

August 22nd, 2020   *New Houston*

My dearest Mina,
Where were you yesterday, I wonder? The ranch, with all its freight of human beings – in which category I include those supernatural beings, our grandchildren – spent yesterday and much of the day before in a benighted bit of somewhere that I presume was medieval Europe! It was our first taste of a major Timeslip. (How easily one takes up the protective jargon – a

Timeslip sounds no worse than a landslide. But you know what I mean – a fault in the spatial infrastructure.)

Now we are all back here in The Present. That term, 'The Present', must be viewed with increasing suspicion as Timeslips increase. But you will understand that I mean the date and hour shown unflinchingly on the calendar-chronometer here in my study. Are we lucky to get back? Could we have remained adrift in time? One of the most terrifying features of this terrifying thing is that so little is understood about it. And in no time at all – I wrote down the phrase unthinkingly – there may be no chance for men of intellect to compare notes.

I can't think straight. Don't expect a coherent letter. It is an absolute shock. The supreme shock outside death. Maybe you have experienced it ... Of course I am wild with anxiety about you. Come home at once, Mina! Then at least we shall be among the Incas or fleeing Napoleon *together!* Reality is going to pot. One thing's for sure – we never had as secure a grasp on reality as we imagine. The only people who can be laughing at present are yesterday's nutcases, the para-psychologists, the junkies, the E.S.P.-buffs, the reincarnationists, the science-fiction writers, and anyone who never quite believed in the homogeneous flow of time.

Sorry. Let me stick to facts.

The ranch got into a timeslip (there's more than one: ours does not merit a capital T). Suddenly we were back – wherever it was.

Sec. of State Dean Reede was with me at the time. I believe I told you last letter that he was coming to see me. Of course, he is firmly in the President's pocket – a Glendale man every inch of him, and as tough as Glendale, as we always knew. He says they will never cease the fight; that all history gives inescapable precedents of how an inferior culture must go down to a superior one. Gives as examples the destruction of Polynesia, the obliteration of the Amazon Indians.

I told him that there was no objective way of judging which side was inferior, which superior: that the Polynesians seemed to have maximized happiness, and that the Indians of the Amazon seemed to be in complete and complex harmony with their environment. That both goals were ones our culture had failed to achieve.

Reede then called me a soft-head, a traitorous liberal (of course I had our conversation played in tape-memory, knowing he would be doing as much). He said that many of the West Powers' present troubles could be blamed on me, because I pursued such a namby-pamby role while acting as presidential advisor. That I should have known that my minor reforms in police rule, housing, work permits, etc., would lead to black revolt. Historically, reform always led to revolt. Etc.

A thoroughly useless and unpleasant argument, but of course I had to defend myself. And I remain sure that history, if there is to be any, will vindicate me. It will certainly have little good to say for Glendale and his hatchetmen. He even had the gall to instance our private picture gallery as an example of my wrong-headedness!

We had got to shouting at each other when the light changed. More than that — the texture of the atmosphere changed. The sky went from its usual washed blue to a dirty grey. There was no shock or jar — nothing like an earth-tremor. But the sensation was so abrupt that both Reede and I ran to the windows.

It was amazing. Cloud was rolling in overhead. Over the plain, coming in fast, was thick mist. In a few moments, it surged over the wall like a sea and burst all over the garden and patio.

And not only that. Ahead, I could see the land stretching as usual, and the low roofs of the old stables. But beyond the roofs, the hills had gone! And to the left, driveway and pampas grass had disappeared. They were replaced by a lumpy piece of country, very green and broken and dotted with green trees — like nowhere in Texas.

'Holy saints! We've been timeslipped!' Reede said. Dazed though I was, I thought how characteristic of him to speak as if this was some personal thing that had been done to *him*. No doubt that was exactly how he saw it.

'I must go to my grandchildren,' I said.

With shrill shouts, Poll and Tony were already running outside. I caught up with them and held their hands, hoping I might be able to protect them from danger. But there was no danger except that most insidious one, the threat to human sanity. We stood there, staring into the mist. Nurse Gregory came out to join us, taking everything with her usual unflustered calm.

When a few minutes had passed, and we were recovering from our first shock, I stepped forward, towards where the drive had been.

'I'd stay where I was, if I was you, Joe,' Reede advised. 'You don't know what might be out there.'

I ignored him. The children were straining to go ahead.

There was a clean line where our sand ended. Beyond it was rank grass, growing as high as the children's knees, and beaded silver with rain. Great shaggy oaks stood everywhere. A path was worn among them.

'I can see a hut over there, Grampy,' Tony said, pointing.

It was a poor affair, built of wood. It had wooden slates on the roof. Behind it was an outhouse, also wooden, and a picket fence, with bushes by it. With an increase in unease, I saw that two people, I thought a man and a woman, stood behind the fence, staring in our direction. I pointed them out to the children.

'Better get back in the house,' Reede advised. 'I'm going to phone the police and see what the hell's happening.' He disappeared.

'They won't hurt us, will they?' said Tony, staring across at the two strangers.

'Not unless we threaten them,' Nurse Gregory said – which I thought was a little optimistic.

'I should imagine they're as startled by us as we are by them,' I said.

Suddenly, the man by the fence turned away and went behind the house. When we next saw him, he was running into the distance, heading uphill. The woman slid out of sight and went into the house.

'Let's have a walk round, Grampy, can we?' Tony said. 'I'd love to go to the top of that hill and see where the man went. Perhaps there's a castle over there.'

It seemed a likely suggestion, but I was too uneasy to leave the relative shelter of our house. I recalled that I had an old-fashioned Colt .45 automatic pistol in my desk; yet the idea of carrying it was repugnant to me. The children kept plaguing me to take them forward. Eventually I gave in. The three of us walked together under the trees, leaving Nurse Gregory to stand on the house side of the danger line.

'Don't go too far,' she called. So she had some sensations of fear!

'No harm will come to us,' I replied. I figured that would reassure all of us.

Well, no harm came to us, but I was in a constant state of worry. Supposing the house snapped back to 2020, leaving us stuck in whatever benighted neck of the woods we had come across? Or supposing – I'm ashamed to put it on paper now – something dreadful came and attacked us, something we didn't know about?

And there was a third worry, shadowy but no pleasanter for that. Supposing that what was happening was just a subjective phenomenon, something going on purely inside my own skull? It was hard to believe that we weren't in a kind of dream.

The kids wanted to go and see if they could see the woman in the wooden house. I made them walk the other way. There was a dog lying inside the picket fence. I had a dread about trying to talk to anyone from – this world, or whatever you should call it.

Poll was the first to see the horseman.

He was riding over the brow of one of the nearby hillocks, accompanied by a man on foot, who held the stirrup with one hand and led a large hound on a leash with the other. They approached slowly, warily, and were still some distance away. All the same, they looked determined; the man on the horse was dressed in tunic and tight trousers, and held a short sword in his hand and wore a curving helmet.

'Pretend you haven't seen them, and we'll walk back to the house,' I said.

Hypocrite! But for the dear children, I would have gone forward to meet him.

The children came along meekly, Poll putting her small hand in mine. Neither of them looked back. We got to the front door, stood on the step and then looked back.

The horseman and his companion came steadily on. The dog strained at its leash. All three of them kept their eyes fixedly on us. When they reached the line where the grass ended and the Texan ground began, they halted.

The horse was a poor spavined creature. The man on the horse looked rather grand. He had a beard and steady dark eyes. His hair and complexion were dark. His attitude was easy in the saddle and expressed determination. The man by his side – I judged it to be the peasant from the wooden house – was a stocky creature whose bodily gestures suggested disquiet.

'Who are you? Do you speak English?' I called.

They just stared back.

'Are you from New Houston?' Tony called bravely.

They made no verbal answer. Instead, the man on horseback raised his sword aloft. In greeting or threat? Then he turned the nag around and, almost sadly, I thought, led back the way he had come.

'I told you they wouldn't hurt us,' Nurse Gregory said, giving me a look of relief.

Tony called once, but they did not turn back, and we watched them until both had disappeared over the brow of the little hill.

You will think this thrilling tale ends in an awful anti-climax, my dear, and be glad that it is so. We never saw those men again. We remained in that timeslip for thirty-five hours or thereabouts, but saw no one else approach.

My anxiety was that the horseman had gone to get re-inforcements. Perhaps there was a castle nearby, as Tony had immediately assumed. I summoned the three serviles and re-programmed them to keep watch – fortunately, I had a defence programme to hand. Reede and I reinforced their watch from time to time, especially during the night, when we also floodlit the house and grounds. I should add that our phones to the outside world were non-functioning but of course the nuclear core supplied us with all the power we needed.

During the night, we heard dogs barking and yapping in the hills. Maybe there were jackals as well. That was all.

This morning, we flipped back into The Present as easily and quietly as we had left it. Here we are, as before – except that the area which returned is not entirely the area which went! I rode round in the buggy this morning, after a brief nap, survey-ing the damage. Nurse Gregory brought the children along and made an outing of it.

You remember what we call the green cottage – the apple

store, beyond the garaging. It has gone. In its place, rough green pasture which will soon wilt in our Texan sun. And where the driveway was we have a line of massive oaks and beeches. The robots are working to clear way between them to the road. Luckily, the road gate is still there – it stayed in 2020 all the while, or so we must assume.

I'm getting one of the oaks sawn down and will dispatch it with soil samples to the Historical Ecology Department at the University. Sitgers there might be able to discover something of its original locality from analysis, though he will never have faced a problem like this before. Where did we go? England? Europe? The Balkans? The guy on the horse was Caucasian. What time was it, what century? I presume it was Earth. Or was it some alternate Earth? Did I stand with the kids on some possible Earth where the year was 2020 and the Industrial Revolution never happened? Am I sheer blind cracked to ask such questions?

When does the next timeslip strike?

You must come back, my dear Mina, if you can get here, war or no war. The war must inevitably fall apart if this schism in the fabric of space/time continues. Come back! The children need their grandmother.

At such a time, I must invoke God and say, God knows, *I* need you!

Your ever-loving husband, JOE

4

CompC Cable from Nurse Gregory to Mrs Mina Bodenland:

August 25th, 2020   *New Houston*

GREATLY REGRET ANNOUNCE DISAPPEARANCE MR JOSEPH BODENLAND DURING BRIEF TIMESLIP DAWN THIS MORNING DURATION TWENTY-FIVE MINUTES STOP POLICE ARE SEARCHING

AREA WITH NEGATIVE RESULTS STOP CHILDREN DISTRESSED
AND ASKING FOR YOU STOP PLEASE INSTRUCT URGENT AND
RETURN NEW HOUSTON URGENT STOP NURSE SHEILA GREGORY
CMPC1535 0825 90IAA593 CI44

5

Extract from W. Central Telecable Record of Conversation
over open phone between Mrs Mina Bodenland and Nurse
Sheila Gregory:

'I hope to be with you by ten thirty tomorrow morning, your
time, if there are no delays in flight schedules as there well
may be. Just give me the details of my husband's disappearance, will you, Nurse?'

'Sure. The timeslip took place at oh-six-forty this morning. It
woke me up and it woke Mr Bodenland up, but the children
stayed asleep. I met him in the hall, and he said, "There's a lake
with mountains behind right outside—" I'd already seen it from
my bedroom. Snow on the mountains and a road by the lake
with a coach being pulled along by two horses.'

'And my husband went out alone?'

'He insisted I stay indoors. I went to the living-room and saw
him drive the Felder out of the garage. He drove into the new
landscape. There was no road, just pasture, and he went very
slowly. Then I couldn't see him any more for a clump of trees
– a wood, I guess it was. I was anxious.'

'Couldn't you have persuaded him to stay indoors?'

'He was determined to go, Mrs Bodenland. You see, my guess
is that he figgered this timeslip would have the same duration
as the last one – a day and a half. Maybe he thought he'd just
drive to the lake and find out where it was – it was a much
pleasanter looking place than the other dump, where the guy
on the horse came to stare at us. I went off to fix myself a
coffee and just as I was coming back, I was entering the living

room and – wham! – the timeslip ceased, just like that, and everything went back to normal. I ran out and called your husband's name but it was no good.'

'Twenty-five minutes, you say?'

'That was all. I came back inside and phoned the police, and then I cabled you. Tony and Polly were real upset when they woke up. They've been crying for you and their Mummy all day, on and off.'

'Tell them I'm on my way home. And please keep them indoors. You've probably heard – organization is breaking down. The world's going plain crazy. Keep the robots programmed for defence.'

Part two

The tape-journal of Joseph Bodenland

I

A record must be kept, for the sanity of all concerned. Luckily, old habits die hard, and I had my tape-memory stowed in the car, together with a stack of other junk. I'll start from the time that darkness came on.

I'd managed to drive over the terrible roads to a village or small town. When I saw buildings coming up, I drove the Felder off the track behind an outcrop of rock, where I hoped it was both safe and unobtrusive for the night. However much of a challenge the town presented, I figured I would cause less stir if I went in on foot than in a four-wheeled horseless vehicle. They did not possess such things here, that was for sure.

All I had to eat was some chocolate Tony had left in the car, washed down by a can of beer in the freeze compartment. My need for a meal and bed overcame my apprehensions.

Although I had kept away from people and villages so far, I knew this was a well inhabited part of the world. I had seen many people in the distance. The scenery was alpine, with broad green valleys surmounted by mountain peaks. More distant were higher peaks, tipped with snow. The bottoms of the valleys contained dashing streams, winding tracks, and picturesque little villages made of pretty wooden houses huddling together. Every village had its church spire; every hour was signalled by a bell chiming in the spires; the sound came clear down the valleys. The mountainsides were strewn with spring flowers. There were cows among the tall grasses – cows with solemn bells about their necks which donged as they moved. Above them, little wooden huts were perched in higher meadows.

It was a beautiful and soothing place. It was just not anything you might encounter in Texas, not if you went back or forward a million years. But it looked mighty like Switzerland.

I know Switzerland well, or did on my own time track.

My years in the American Embassy in Brussels had been well spent. I learnt to speak French and German fluently, and had passed as much leave as I could travelling about Europe. Switzerland had become my favourite country. At one time I had bought a chalet just outside Interlaken.

So I walked into the town. A board on the outskirts gave its name as Sècheron and listed times of Holy Mass. Overhanging balconies, neat piles of kindling wood against every wall. A rich aroma of manure and wood smoke, pungent to my effete nostrils. And a sizeable inn which, with antique lettering, proclaimed itself to be the Hôtel Dejean. The exterior was studded with chamoix horns and antlers of deer.

What gave me a thrill – why, outside the low door, two men were unloading something from a cart; it was the carcass of a bear! I had never seen that before. What was more, I could understand what the men were saying; although their accents were strange, their French was perfectly comprehensible.

As soon as I entered a cheerful low room with oil lamps burning, I was greeted by the host. He asked me a lot of suspicious questions, and eventually I was shown to what must have been the poorest room in his house, over the kitchen, facing a hen-run. It mattered not to me. A servant girl brought me up water, I washed and lay back on the bed to rest before dinner. I slept.

When I woke, it was without any idea of time. The timeslip had upset my circadian rhythms. I knew only that it was dark, and had been for some while. I lay there in a sort of wonderment, listening to a rich world of sound about me. The great wooden chalet creaked and resonated like a galleon in full sail. I could hear the voices of the wood, and human voices, as well as snatches of song and music. Somewhere, cowbells sounded;

the animals had been brought in for the night, maybe. And there was that wonderful world of smells! You might say that the thought uppermost in my mind was this: Joe Bodenland, you have escaped the twenty-first century!

My sleep had done something for me. Earlier in the day, I had been close to despair. Driving the Felder, I looked back towards the ranch and found it had disappeared. I had left it only twenty minutes earlier. In complete panic, I turned the car around and drove back to where the house had been. I knew exactly where it stood because one of our pampas bushes was there and, in the middle of it, a coloured ball of Tony's. Nothing else. The ranch, the children, all had snapped back to their normal time.

Blackest despair – now total euphoria! I was a different man, full of strength and excitement. Something the innkeeper had said when I made apologies for possessing no luggage had begun to tip my mood.

'General Bonaparte has a lot to answer for. He may be safely out of the way again now, but a lot of decent people have no safety and no homes.'

He had taken me for some kind of refugee from the Napoleonic Wars! They had finished in 1815, with Napoleon's banishment to St Helena. So the date was some time shortly after that.

You think I could take such knowledge calmly? Mina, will you ever hear these tapes? Don't you see, as far as I knew, I was the first man ever to be displaced in time, though no doubt the timeslips were now making a regular thing of it. I remembered reading the old nursery classic, Herbert Wells's *The Time Machine*, but Wells's time-traveller had gone ahead in time. How much nicer to go back. The past was safe!

I was back in history! Something had come over me. Rising from the bed, I felt curiously unlike myself. Or rather, I could feel the old cautious Bodenland inside, but it seemed as if a new man, fitted for decision and adventure, had taken control of me. I went downstairs to demand supper.

Men were drinking there by a fire, beneath a cuckoo-clock. There were tables, two empty, two occupied. One of the occupied tables contained a man and woman and child, tucking in to great slabs of meat. At the other occupied table sat a lean-visaged but elegant man in dark clothes, reading a paper by candle-light as he ate.

Ordinarily, I would have chosen an empty table. In my new mood, I went over to the solitary man and said easily, pulling out a chair, 'May I sit at your table?'

For a moment I thought my accent had not been understood. Then he said, 'I can't stop you sitting here,' and lowered his head to his paper again.

I sat down. The innkeeper's daughter came across to me, and offered me a choice of trout or venison. I ordered trout with white wine to accompany it. She was back promptly with a chilled wine and bread rolls with crisp brown crust and thick doughy interior, which I broke and ate with covert greed. How heady was my excitement, tasting that historic food!

'May I offer you a glass of wine?' I said to my table companion. He had an earthenware jug of water by his side.

He looked up and studied me again. 'You may offer, sir, and I may refuse. The social contract countenances both actions!'

'My action may be more mutually beneficial than yours.'

Maybe my answer pleased him. He nodded, and I summoned the girl to bring another wine glass.

My hesitant companion said, 'May I drink to your health without necessarily wishing to listen to your conversation? You will think me discourteous, but perhaps I may excuse myself by explaining that it is the discourtesy of grief.'

'I'm sorry to hear that. To hear that you have cause for grief, I mean. Some find distraction welcome at such times.'

'Distraction? All my life I have been a man who scorned distraction! There's work to be done in the world – so much to be found out—' He checked himself abruptly, lifted his glass at me and took a sip from it.

How good that wine tasted, if only because I secretly thought, what a rare old vintage I must be quaffing, laid down no doubt before the Battle of Trafalgar!

I said, 'I am older than you, sir (how easily that polite "sir" crept in as a mode of address!) – old enough to discover that finding out often leads to less pleasurable states of mind than mere ignorance!'

At that he laughed curtly. 'That I find an ignorant point of view. I perceive nevertheless that you are a man of culture, and a foreigner. Why do you stay in Sècheron and deny yourself the pleasures of Geneva?'

'I like the simple life.'

'I should be in Geneva now ... I arrived there too late, after sunset, and found the gates of the city shut, confound it. Otherwise I'd be at my father's house ...'

Again an abrupt halt to his speech. He frowned and stared down at the grain of the table. I longed to ask questions but was wary of revealing my complete lack of local knowledge.

The girl brought me soup and then my trout, the best and freshest I had ever tasted, though the potatoes that accompanied it were not so good. *No refrigeration,* I thought; *not a can to be found throughout the land!* A shock went through me. Cultural shock. Temporal shock.

My companion took this opportunity to hide himself in his papers. So I listened to the talk of the travellers about me, hoping for a bit of instant history. But were they talking about the aftermath of the Napoleonic Wars? Were they talking about the increasing industrialization of the times? Were they talking about the first steamship crossing the Atlantic? Were they talking about Walter Scott or Lord Byron or Goethe or Metternich? Were they talking about the slave trade or the Congress of Vienna? (All matters which I judged to be vital and contemporary!) Did they spare one word for that valiant new American nation across the Atlantic?

They did not.

They talked about the latest sensation – some wretched murder – and about a woman, a maidservant, who was to be tried for the murder in Geneva the next day! I would have sighed for human nature, had it not been for the excellence of my trout and the wine which accompanied it.

At last, as I set my knife and fork down, I caught the gloomy eye of my table-companion and ventured to say, 'You will be in Geneva tomorrow in time to see this wretched woman brought to justice, I presume?'

His face took on severe lines, anger glowed in his eyes. Setting his papers down, he said in a low voice, 'Justice, you say? What do you know of the case that you prejudge this lady's guilt beforehand? Why should you be so anxious that she should hang? What injury did she ever do you – or any living soul, for that matter?'

'I must apologize – I see you know the lady personally.'

But he had dropped his eyes and lost interest in me. Shrinking back in his chair, he seemed to become prey to some inner conflict. 'About her head hangs purest innocence. Deepest guilt lies heavy on the shoulders...' I did not catch his last words; perhaps he said, '... of others'.

I rose, bid him good evening, and went outside to stand in the road and enjoy the scents of darkness and the sight of the moon. Yes, I stood in the middle of the road, and gloried that there was no danger of being knocked down by traffic.

The sound of a running stream invited me over to a bridge. Standing there in shade, I observed the man and woman who had also been eating in the hotel emerge with their child.

He said, 'I wonder if Justine Moritz will sleep peacefully tonight!' They both chuckled and passed on down the road.

Justine Moritz! I divined that they spoke of the woman who was on trial for her life in Geneva on the morrow. More! I had heard that name before, and searched my memory to discover its associations. I recalled de Sade's heroine, Justine, and reflected that he too would be alive now, if *now* was when I believed it to be. But my new superior self told me that Justine Moritz was somebody else.

As I stood with my hands resting on the stone of the bridge, the door of the hotel was again thrown open. A figure emerged, pulling a cloak about him. It was my melancholy friend. An accordion sounded within the hotel, and I guessed that the distractions of music might have driven him outside.

His movements suggested as much. He paced about with arms folded. Once, he threw them wide in a gesture of protest. He looked in every way a man distraught. Although I felt sorry for him, that prickliness in his manner made me reluctant to reveal myself.

Of a sudden, he made up his mind. He said something aloud – something about a devil, I thought – and then he began striding away as if his life depended on it.

My superior self came to an immediate decision. Normally, I would have returned indoors and gone meekly to bed. Instead, I began to follow my distraught friend at a suitable distance.

The way he went led downhill. The road curved, and I emerged from a copse to confront a splendid panorama. There was the lake — Lake Geneva, Lac Léman, as the Swiss call it — and there, not far distant, lay the spires and roofs of Geneva!

It was a city I had loved in my time. Now, how it was shrunken! The moonlight lent it enchantment, of course, but what a pokey place it looked, lying by the lakeside in the clear night. Romantic behind its walls, yes, but nothing to the great city I had known. In my day — why, Sècheron would have been swallowed up by inner suburbs clustering round the old U.N. building.

But my superior self made nothing of that. We moved down the hill, my quarry and I. There was a village clinging to the lakeside. Somewhere lay the sound of singing — I say *lay* for the voice seemed to float on the waters as gently as a slight mist.

My friend went on down the winding road for about two miles, finishing at the quayside, where he rapped smartly on a door. I hung about further down the street, hoping not to be seen by the few people who were strolling there. I watched as he engaged a man who led him down to a boat; they climbed in, and the man began to haul away on his oars. The boat slipped through shadow and then, could be seen heading across the lake, already slightly obscured by the tenuous mist. Without thinking, I went to the edge of the quay.

At once a man came up to me bearing a dim lantern and said, 'Are you requiring a ferry to the other side of the lake, good sir?'

Why not? The chase was on. In no time, we had arranged terms. We climbed down to his fishing boat and were pushing off against the stonework. I told him to dowse his lantern and follow the other boat.

'I expect you are acquainted with the gentleman in the other vessel, sir,' my oarsman said.

These villagers — of course they would make it their business to know anyone who was rich and whose father lived so near! Here was the chance to have my suspicions confirmed.

'I know his name,' I said boldly. 'But I'm surprised you should!'

'The family is well-known in these parts, good sir. He is young Victor Frankenstein, his famous father's son.'

2

Frankenstein's boat moored at the Plainpalais Quay, on the other side of sleeping Geneva. In my day, the area formed part of the centre of that city. It was but a village, and four small sailing boats, sails drooping and oars plying, moved out from a tiny wooden jetty as we moved in.

Telling him to wait, I followed Frankenstein at a distance. Can you imagine what my excitement was? I assume you cannot, for already the feelings I had at the time are inscrutable to me, so imbued was I with an electric sense of occasion. My superior self had taken over – call it the result of time-shock, if you will, but I felt myself in the presence of myth and, by association, *accepted myself as mythical!* It is a sensation of some power, let me tell you! The mind becomes simple and the will strong.

Frankenstein, *the* Frankenstein, walked briskly, and I followed briskly. Despite the peace of the early night, lightning was flickering about the horizon. Horizon may be an appropriate word in Texas, but it does no justice to the country beyond Plainpalais, for there the horizon includes Mont Blanc, the highest mountain in the Alps, or in Europe, for that matter. The lightning bathed the peak in intricate figures, which seemed to grow brighter as clouds rolled up and hid the moon. At first, the lightning was silent, almost furtive; then peals of thunder accompanied it.

The thunder helped to camouflage the noise of my steps. We were now climbing fairly steeply into the mountains and silence was impossible if I were not to lose my quarry. He paused at one point on a low hill and cried aloud – perhaps not without a touch of relish for the dramatic, characteristic of his age – 'William, dearest little brother! Close by this spot wast thou murdered and thy dear innocence cast down!'

He raised his hands. Then he said, more soberly, 'And the guilt rests with me . . .' and lowered his arms to his side.

I should be more particular in my description of this singular man. A side-view of his face was reminiscent of profiles seen on coins and medals, for his features were clear-cut and sharp.

And one has to have some distinction to appear on a medal. This clarity, aided by his youth, made him handsome, though there was about the handsomeness something of the coldness of a coin. His features were a little too set. The melancholy that had struck me at first was very much a part of his character.

Rain began to fall in large heavy drops. As I recalled, storms spring up rapidly about the Swiss lakes, appearing to arrive from all corners of the sky at once. The thunder burst with a grand crash above our heads, and the heavens flung down their contents upon us.

Over to the north-west, the dark bulk of the Jura was flickeringly lit. The lake became an intermittent sheet of fire. The heavy clouds that had gathered about the summit of Mont Blanc boiled from within. The world was full of noise, dazzling light, blinding darkness, torrential rain.

All of which served merely to raise Frankenstein's spirits. He walked more briskly now, still climbing, picking his way fast and carelessly, so that he could keep his face turned up as much as possible to the source of the storm.

He was shouting aloud. Much of what he said was lost in the noise, but once, as we climbed a precipitous path and were no more than four metres apart, I heard him cry aloud the name of William again. 'William, my dear little angel! This is thy funeral, this thy dirge!'

With similar cries, he staggered out on to more level ground. I was about to break from sheltering rock and follow when I saw him stop aghast and raise one arm involuntarily in a gesture of self-protection.

In that broken place, rocks and shattered boulders lay in a half-circle, ruinous pines growing among them. My immediate thought was that Frankenstein had encounted a bear, and might at any moment come dashing back and discover me. Blunderingly, I moved to my left among the boulders, being careful to keep behind them and not be seen. Then, crouching down, I peered out through the pouring rain and saw such a sight as I will never forget.

Frankenstein was backing away, still holding that defensive gesture. His jaw hung open, and he was near enough for me to see the rain dashing from his face – when lightning showed him at all. Before him, a monstrous shape had emerged from a clump of shattered pines.

It was no bear. In most respects it was human in shape, but gigantic in stature, and there seemed nothing of the human being in the way it suddenly paced forward from the trees. The lightning came again, and a tremendous stroke of thunder. I was staring at Frankenstein's monster!

As if to increase my terror, there came at that instant a pause in the electric war overhead. Only far away among the trees did a flickering still galvanize the distant Jura. We were cast into impenetrable blackness, with the rain still cascading down and that devilish thing on the loose!

I slipped limply to my knees in extreme terror, still staring ahead, never daring even to blink, though the rain poured down my forehead and over my staring eyeballs.

There was another streak of lightning overhead. Frankenstein had slumped back against a tree-trunk for support, his head lolling back as if he were about to collapse in a faint. His monster, the creature he had created, was striding towards him. Then blackness again.

Then more lightning. The gigantic figure had passed by Frankenstein as if the latter did not exist. But it was coming towards me. I saw that its arms did not swing properly as it walked – but, oh, how fast it walked!

Another great peal of thunder, then more lightning. The abominable thing took a tremendous leap. It was above me on the rocks, and then it sprang into the darkness behind me. For a moment I heard its footsteps in something between a walk and a run, then it was gone. I was left crouching in the rain.

After a while, I pulled myself together and stood up. The storm seemed to be moving over a little. Frankenstein still leaned against the tree, bereft of movement.

During one flash of lightning, I saw a refuge, standing some way behind me. I could take the rain no longer. I was frozen, although the weather had only a half-share in that. As I headed towards shelter, I glanced south, where the broad shoulders of a mountain – its name is Mont Salève – stood against the troubled sky. There I saw the monster again, swarming up the cruel face. It went like a spider, climbing almost perpendicularly. It was superhuman.

I burst into the hut, gasping and shuddering, and stripped off jacket, shirt, and undervest. Between chattering teeth, I was talking to myself.

In the hut were a wooden bed, a stove, a table, and rope. A rough blanket lay neatly folded on the bed. I snatched it up and flung it round me, sitting there shaking.

Gradually, the rain petered out. A wind blew. All was silence, save for the dripping roof outside. The lightning ceased. My trembling ceased. My earlier excitement returned.

I – I – had seen Frankenstein's monster! There was no mistaking it.

Of its face I had no clear idea. The twenty-first century 4-D representations had prepared me for something horrific; yet my impression was of features more frightening than strictly horrifying. I could not recall the face. The light was so confusing, the monster's movements so fast, that I had a memory only of an abstraction of sculptured bone. The overall impression had been fully as alarming as anyone could have anticipated. Its creator's reaction to it had merely added to my alarm.

Putting on my wet clothes, I moved out of the hut.

I had thought the moonlight was diffused through cloud, so general was the dim light. Once I was outside, however, I saw that the sky was almost free of cloud and the moon had set. Dawn was breaking over the world once more.

Victor Frankenstein was still in the clearing where I had last seen him. As if immune to discomfort and pain, he stood in his damp cloak with one foot up on a stone. Resting his weight on his bended knee, he was staring motionless over a precipice towards the lake. What he looked at inwardly, I know not. But his immobility, long maintained, hinted at the heaviness of his thoughts, and lent him something of the awe that attached to his odious creation.

I was about to make quietly down the hillside when he moved. Slowly, he shook his head once or twice, and then began to make the descent. Since daylight was flooding into the world, I was able to stay at a distance and keep him in sight. So we both came down from the mountain. Truth was, I more than once looked back over my shoulder to see if anything was following me.

The gates of Geneva were open. Wagons were going out empty, heading for the forest. I saw a spanking stage emerge and take the road that led to Chamonix, its four horses stepping high. Frankenstein entered between the grey walls, and I ceased to follow him.

3

This record so far has been dictated in one long burst. After watching Victor Frankenstein walk towards his father's house, I came through Geneva and back to Sècheron and my auto-mobile. The Felder was as I had left it; I climbed in and put this account in my portable tape-memory.

My heart-searchings must have no place here. Before getting to the murder trial, I will note two incidents that occurred in Geneva. Two things I wanted above all, and one of them was money, for I knew old systems of currency were in operation throughout the nineteenth century. The second thing I found quickly by looking at a newspaper in a coffee-shop: the day's date. It was May 23rd, 1816.

I scanned the paper for news. It was disappointingly empty of anything I could comprehend; mainly there was local news, with a great deal of editorializing about the German Constitution. The name of Carl August of Saxe-Weimar figured largely, but I had heard neither of him nor of it. Perhaps I had naively expected headlines of the HUMPHRY DAVY INVENTS MINERS' SAFETY LAMP, ROSSINI WRITES FIRST OPERA, HENRY THOREAU BORN, kind of thing! At least the newspaper's editorial columns served to remind me that Geneva had become part of Switzer-land only in the previous year.

My quest for money also held its disappointments. I had on my wrist – besides my CompC phone, now useless – a new disposable watch, powered by a uranium isotope and worth at least seventy thousand dollars at current going price in U.S.A., 2020. As a unique object in Geneva, 1816, how much greater should its value be! Moreover, the Swiss watchmakers were the best equipped in the world at this time to appreciate its sophistication.

Full of hope, I took the watch in to a smart business in the Rue du Rhône, where it was examined by a stately manager.

'How do you open it?' he asked.

'It won't open. It is sealed shut.'

'Then how does one examine the works if something goes wrong?'

'That is the whole virtue of this particular make of watch. It does not go wrong. It is guaranteed never to go wrong!'

He smiled very charmingly at me.

'Certainly its defects are very well concealed. So too is the winder!'

'Ah, but it does not wind. It will go forever – or at least for a century. Then it stops, and one throws it away. It is a disposable watch.'

His smile grew still sweeter. He looked at my clothes, all creased and still damp from the night's activities. 'I observe you are a foreigner, m'sieu. I presume this is a foreign watch. From the Netherlands, perhaps?'

'It's North Korean,' I said.

With the tenderest of smiles, he proferred my watch to me in an open palm. 'Then may I suggest you sell your unstoppable watch back to the North Koreans, m'sieu!'

At two other establishments I had no better luck. But at a fourth I met an inquisitive little man who took greatly to the instrument, examining it under magnifying glasses and listening to its working through a miniature stethoscope.

'Very ingenious, even if it is powered by a bee who will expire as you leave my premises!' he said. 'Where was it made?'

'It's the latest thing from North America.' I was learning caution.

'Such a timepiece! What is this "N.K." inscribed on its face?'

'It stands for New Kentucky.'

'I have not even seen this metal before. It interests me, and I shall have pleasure taking it apart and examining its secrets.'

'Those secrets could set you a century ahead of all rival watchmakers.'

We began arguing over prices. In the end, I accepted a

derisory sum, and left his shop feeling sore and cheated. Yet, directly I stepped out into the sunshine again, my superior self took over, and I looked at the matter differently. I had good solid francs in my pocket, and what did the watchmaker have? A precision instrument whose chief virtues were useless to anyone in this age. Its undeviating accuracy in recording the passage of time to within one twenty-millionth of a second was a joke in a world that still went largely by the leisurely passage of the sun, where stage-coaches left at dawn, noon, or sunset. That wretched obsession with time which was a hallmark of my own age had not yet set in; there were not even railway timetables to make people conform to the clock.

As for the workings of the watch, there was another item this world was mercifully without: uranium. That element had been a twentieth-century discovery and, within a few years of its first refinement, had been used in new and more powerful weapons of destruction.

Even in the United States of Korea – in my day, one of the foremost manufacturing countries of the world, with the deepest mantle-mines – in 1816, the peoples of the Korean peninsula would be painting exquisite scenes on silk and carving delicate ivory. Between slaying each other by the sword, admittedly, in preparation for more energetic centuries to come . . .

The more I thought about it, the shedding of my watch became symbolic, and I rejoiced accordingly.

If I was learning about time, I was also learning about my legs. They brought me through the city and back to Sècheron in good order. I had not walked so far for years.

I'm in the automobile now, my last little bastion of the twenty-first century. It is uranium-powered too. I returned to the spot where my home once stood, looked affectionately at Tony's bright plastic ball in the knot of pampas, and left a plastic message pad beside it with a message for Mina, in case the area does a timeslip again and she happens to be there.

This brings my record up-to-date. I must sleep before relating what happened at the murder trial. I am fit and charged with excitement, beside myself in a strangely literal way. Maybe it is obvious what I shall be compelled to do next.

4

Before I describe the trial of Justine Moritz, I must set down what I know about Frankenstein, in the hope of clarifying my mind.

The little I know is little enough. Victor Frankenstein is the eponymous central character of a novel by Mary Shelley. He amalgamated parts of human bodies to create a 'monster', which he then brought to life. The monster wreaked destruction on him and his house. Among the general public, the name of creator and created became confused.

I remember reading the novel as a child, when it made a great impression on me, but the deplorable pastiches and plagiarizations put out by the mass media have obliterated my memory of the original details. Although I know that the novel was published in the nineteenth century, the actual date escapes me. The author was Mary Shelley, wife of the Romantic poet Percy Bysshe Shelley, but very little of her life comes back to memory. Also, I had the impression that Victor Frankenstein was purely an invented character; however, recent events have somewhat shaken my preconceptions of probability!

From the first moment I set eyes on Frankenstein, at the hotel in Sècheron, I had the impression of a man with a burdensome secret. After selling my watch, I thought further about him, and perceived a link between his past and my future. The aspirations of the society of my day were mirrored in miniature in that watch: the desire that it should never need maintenance, should never run down. Such were Victor Frankenstein's perfectionist obsessions in relation to human anatomy, when he began his investigations into the nature of life. When he reflected on how age and death laid waste man's being, and saw a means of interfering with that process, he acted as harbinger to the Age of Science then in its first dawn.

Was that not the whole burden of his song, that nature needed in some way to be put to rights, and that it was man's job to see it was put to rights? And had not that song passed like a plague virus to every one of his fellow men in succeeding generations? My supremely useless watch, product of endless refinement and research, target of envy for those who did not possess one, was a small example of how his diseased mentality had triumphed. The Conquest of Nature – the loss of man's inner self!

You see the leaps my mind takes. I lived but one day of the spring in 1816 and I was full of love for it – and of hate for what man had done to change that sturdy and natural order.

Even as I say it, I know my statement to be sentimental and truth to be more complex than that. To regard the people and society of 1816 as 'better' than those of my day would be a mistake. For I had already sat through a grave miscarriage of justice.

The trial of Justine Moritz began at eleven. The court was packed. I managed to get a fairly good seat, and it was my fortune to sit next to a man who delighted in explaining the nuances of the case to a foreigner.

He pointed out to me the benches where the Frankenstein family sat. They were noticeable enough. While the rest of the courtroom was filled with excited anticipation, covert but gloating, the faces of the Frankensteins were all gloomy. They could have been members of the House of Atreus.

First came old syndic Alphonse Frankenstein, bent of shoulder, grey of hair; but his gaze, as he looked about the court, was still commanding. As my companion informed me, he had held many important posts in Geneva, and was a counsellor, as his father and grandfather had been before him.

The counsellor was consoled by Elizabeth Lavenza, who sat next to him. I thought she was startlingly beautiful, even in her grief, with her fair hair tucked under a dainty mourning bonnet, and her slim upright figure. She had been adopted as a small child by the counsellor's wife, now dead – so said my companion, adding that it was well known that she would marry Victor, and so come into a deal of money. She had instigated a series of protracted lawsuits in her own right with authorities in Milan, Vienna and a German city, trying to reclaim a fortune supposedly left her by a defecting father. Maybe news of these extensive litigations, as well as her beauty, drew many pairs of eyes towards where she sat.

Victor sat on her other side. He was pale and composed at first, his features rigidly set. He held his head defiantly lifted, as if he wished no man to see him in dejection; somehow I felt the gesture very characteristic, and was able for the first time to recognize his arrogance.

Next to Victor was his brother Ernest, slender and rather dandyish in his dress although, like the rest of his family, he was in deep mourning. Ernest fidgeted and looked about him, occasionally addressing remarks to his elder brother, which Victor made no noticeable attempt to answer. The two brothers were present in court because of the foul murder of their younger brother, William, who had been found strangled.

'Poor little lad, only six-and-a-half years old!', said my companion. 'They do say he was sexually assaulted, but the family's trying to keep it hushed up.'

'If that was so, surely his nurse would not have tampered with him.'

'Oh, she did it right enough, make no mistake about that! The evidence all points to it. You never know about people nowadays, do you?'

'Where was the child murdered? At home?'

'No, no, outside the city, up in the hills, where he was playing with his brother Ernest. Out by Plainpalais, towards Mont Salève.'

Then I understood more fully Frankenstein's quest in the storm of the previous night! He had been seeking out the spot on which his little brother was strangled – and we had encountered the murderer there.

Waves of cold ran over me, over my flesh and through my body. I thought I was about to faint, and could pay no attention as my companion pointed out the Clervals, a wealthy merchant family, of whom Henry Clerval was a close friend of Victor's; Duvillard, a rich banker, and his new wife; Louis Manoir; and many other local notables. Victor turned once, to nod to Henry Clerval.

What struck me about the Frankensteins was their youth, the father excepted, of course. Set-faced though he was, Victor was certainly not more than twenty-five, and Elizabeth probably younger, while Ernest was still in his mid-teens.

When Justine Moritz was led into the box, I saw that she also was extremely young. A rather plain girl, but with the radiance of youth on her face, though that radiance was well subdued by her present predicament. She spoke up properly when questioned.

I cannot go into the whole trial; time is too short. Despite excellent character-witnesses, among them Elizabeth, who delivered an impassioned plea on her maid's behalf, Justine stood condemned by one piece of circumstantial evidence: a locket containing a picture of her late mistress had been found in her belongings — a locket which the child William had been wearing only the day before the murder. The girl could not explain how the locket came to be among her clothes, and it was clear that her protestations of innocence were in vain. The feeling of the court was almost a tangible thing: something vile had happened and someone had to pay for it. Justine was captive: Justine must pay.

Tremors of horror were still racking me. For only I and one other person in that courtroom knew the truth, knew that the hand which had dispatched William had been neither a female hand nor a male one, but the hand of a terrible neuter thing!

My gaze went frequently to the other bearer of that awful secret. Whereas Elizabeth was composed, though pale, Victor became increasingly nervous, rubbing his forehead and his lips with a handkerchief, hiding his eyes in his palms, staring about in a distraught fashion.

Would he rise and declare his knowledge? But what could he say that would find credence here? Nobody else had seen his monster! Such a tale as he would have to tell would be instantly dismissed, the court being in the frame of mind it was. As well might I have risen and said, 'I will tell you what really happened, for this trial and the real issues involved will one day become the subject of a great novel, and I am a man from two centuries into your future who read that book as a lad...'

Preposterous! But the temptation to intervene grew nevertheless, particularly as I saw things turning against the innocent maidservant.

Victor could bear it no longer. There was a scuffle and he stood up, pushed past brother and friends, and dashed from the courtroom.

Elizabeth stood up, a commanding little figure with one hand half-extended, and watched him go. The proceedings continued.

When all had been said that could be said, the judge made a brief summary, the ballots were cast, and the verdict was solemnly delivered. Justine Moritz was found guilty of the murder of William Frankenstein, and was sentenced to be hanged within the space of two days.

5

If the phrase is not inappropriate here, there was no time to be lost. I tied a tarpaulin over the car and paid a farmer with a horse to drag it through the streets of the city and out to the Plainpalais gate. Fortunately, the good citizens of Geneva had enough else to think about at this juncture.

I knew that there was one place, and one place only – and there one person only – to which I might turn for help!

When I had paid the farmer off, I started my car, my remaining outpost of another century, and drove along a road which led close to the lake. Little I cared then who saw me. My superior self was on a quixotic errand!

Quixotic or not, I had no real idea of where I was going. Or rather, I had an idea, but it was of the vaguest. Far more clear in my mind were recurrent pictures of Victor trembling as if with fever; Elizabeth, fair and beautiful and composed; Justine, pleading without effect for her life before a room full of people covertly eager for her blood; and the creature Frankenstein had made – that gigantic figure without a face, striking fear and worse than fear wherever it went. Although I knew it moved rapidly, all I had of it in my memory was a series of still pictures, captured in rain by lightning. It was enemy to the world, yet the world knew nothing of it! What a madman Frankenstein was to have created such a thing, and to hope to keep its existence a secret!

I tried to recall details of Frankenstein's ghastly history. How would he act if he knew that his career was to be made into fiction, to serve as an object lesson, and a name of opprobrium, to the generations that followed him? Unfortunately, I had not read Mary Shelley's novel since I was a lad; such recollection of it as I had was obscured by the travesties of it I had watched in 4-D on film, TV, and CircC.

At this juncture, I realized that I had driven close to the point where the boat had landed me the previous evening. I was not far from where the boy William had been murdered. I stopped the car.

There were binoculars in the Felder. Nor had I forgotten the swivel-gun mounted on the roof. The thought that such armament was compulsory for anyone privileged enough to own a private car in my own time reminded me that, Napoleonic Wars apart, I was now in an age where the safety and sanctity of the individual was taken for granted. If you read this, Mina, no doubt you will realize what was in my mind; supernaturally fast Frankenstein's creation might be, but the swivel-gun would stop him.

Through the binoculars, I traced the path I had taken the night before when following Victor.

As I half-expected, Victor had returned to the scene of his younger brother's murder. No doubt he had fled straight there from the pressures of the court. I could not see him well; he was mainly hidden behind trees, and motionless. Although I scanned the terrain round about him anxiously, I could discover no sign of the monster.

Locking the car, I began to climb the hill.

So far, I have evaded a central issue. Now it was forced on me. The accidents that had brought me back into the past were real enough. My whole being accepted the fact that I was, *at least in some fashion*, in Switzerland in the year 1816, in the month of May.

But Frankenstein? He was a fictitious character, a myth, wasn't he? There was no way that I could understand whereby he could exist. The fact that *I* was where I was might be highly unlikely; that did not make *his* being there any more likely. In fact, I had to admit it. I found his existence impossible to explain. Although I was about to confront him, my experience told me that he was – well, I've no words for it: on a different plane of reality.

At last I was up on a level with him. The lake was below, the dull tinkle of cowbells came up to me. A peaceful enough spot, yet made profoundly melancholy by reason of its associations. The trees in their light spring foliage held no cheer.

Frankenstein was walking to and fro now, muttering to himself. In my hesitation to step forth lay this question : supposing that this encounter revealed my unreality rather than his ...? As I was about to move forward, a whole cloud of doubt precipitated itself upon me. The frail web of human perceptions was laid bare. I stood outside myself and saw myself there, a poor creature whose energies were based on a slender set of assumptions, whose very identity was a chancy affair of chemicals and accidents.

'Who's there? Come forth if you still haunt this place, damned being!'

Maybe I had made some inadvertent noise. Victor was confronting me, his face white and drawn. I saw no fear there.

I stood forth.

'Who are you, and what do you want with me? Are you from the court?'

'Monsieur Frankenstein, my name is Bodenland, Joseph Bodenland. We met at the hotel yesterday. I apologize for intruding upon you.'

'No matter, if you have news. Is a verdict out yet?'

'Yes.' I had recovered myself by now. 'Justine has been condemned to death. The verdict was the inevitable one in view of your silence.'

'What do you know of my affairs? Who sent you here?'

'I am here on my own account. And I know little of your affairs, except the one crucial thing which nobody else seems to know – the central secret of your life!'

He was still confronting me in a pugnacious attitude, but at this he took a step back.

'Are you another phantom sent to plague me? A product of my imagination?'

'You are sick, man! Because of your sickness, an innocent woman is going to die, and your fair Elizabeth is going to be plunged into misery.'

'Whoever or whatever you are, you speak truth. Unhappy wretch that I am, I left my native fireside and alienated my home to seek strange truths in undiscovered lands. My responsibility is too great, too great!'

41

'Then you must yield some of it to others. Go before the syndics of Geneva and declare your error. They will then do their best to right what has gone wrong: at the least, they can set Justine free. It's useless to come up here and luxuriate in your sins!'

He had been wringing his hands. Now he looked up angrily. 'Who are you to charge me with that? Luxuriate, you say! What do you know of my inner torment? Rendered all the worse by the high hopes I once had, the desire to wrest from Mother Nature some of her deepest secrets, however dark the passage down which I might tread. What cared I for myself? Truth was everything to me! I wanted to improve the world, to deliver into man's hands some of those powers which had hitherto been ascribed to a snivelling and fictitious God! I made my bed in charnels and on coffins, that a new Promethean fire might be lit! What man ever achieved what I have achieved? And you speak of my *sins!*'

'Why not? Isn't your ambition itself a sin? You admitted your own guilt, didn't you?'

His manner became less wild. Almost contemplatively, he said, 'Since I am an atheist and do not believe in God, I do not believe in sin in the sense you intend the word. Nor do I believe that the zeal of discovery is a cause for shame. But guilt I believe in, Oh yes! I sometimes think that guilt is a permanent condition with me and, possibly, with all men in their secret hearts. Perhaps religions have been invented to try to exorcize that condition. It is guilt, not age or misunderstanding, that withers cheeks and drives friends and lovers apart.

'Yet why should this condition be? Whence does it come? Is it a modern thing? From now onwards, are all generations to feel guilty? Because man's powers grow, generation by generation. So much have we achieved, so much more is there to achieve. Must that achievement always carry the maggot of guilt in it?

'Or perhaps guilt has always been a condition of man, since the early days of the world, before time rolled out like a long slumber across the universe. Perhaps it is to do with the nature of his conception, and with the lustful coming together of man and woman.'

'Why do you suppose that?'

'Because that intense pleasure which procreation gives is the moment when human beings shed their humanity and become as the animals, mindless, sniffing, licking, grunting, copulating ... My new creation was to be free of all that. No animal origins, no guilt ...'

With his hand, he covered his eyes and his brow.

'You have a singularly repulsive view of humanity,' I said. 'Is this perhaps why you will do nothing to save Justine?'

'I cannot go to the syndics. I cannot!'

'At least tell the woman whom you love. There must be trust between you!'

'Tell Elizabeth? I would die of shame! I have not even confided in Henry, and he was a student with me at Ingoldstadt, when I began my experiments! No, what I have done myself, I must undo myself. Leave me now, whoever or whatever you are. I have said things to you, Bodenland, which I have said to no man; see that they repose in you as securely as in a grave. I am discomposed, or I would not speak as I have. I mean to arm myself from this day on – be warned, lest you are tempted to trespass on my confidence. Now, I pray, leave me.'

'Very well. If you will confide in nobody else, then you know what you must do.'

'Leave me, I asked you! You know nothing of my problems! – Wait, one commission you could do for me!'

'Ask me!'

He looked somewhat shame-faced. 'For good reasons which you may or may not understand, I desire to remain here in the wilderness, away from those to whom I may inadvertently bring catastrophe. Take, I beg you, a word of explanation to Elizabeth Lavenza, my betrothed.'

All his movements were impatient. Without waiting for my assent, he pulled writing materials from his cloak, where I saw he had several notebooks. He ripped a page from one of them. Turning, he leaned against a rock and scribbled a few sentences – with the air of a man signing his own death warrant, I thought.

'There!' He folded it. 'I can trust you to deliver it unread?'

'Most certainly.' I hesitated, but he turned away. His mind was already elsewhere.

6

I went on foot to the house of the Frankensteins. It was an imposing mansion standing in one of Geneva's central streets and overlooking the Rhône. When I asked to speak for a moment with Miss Lavenza, a manservant showed me into a living-room and asked me to wait.

To be there! Victor was right to wonder what I was. I no longer knew myself. My identity was becoming more and more tenuous. It would be the way of our century to say that I was suffering from time-shock, no doubt; since our personality is largely built and buttressed by our environment, and the assumptions environment and society force upon us, one has but to tip away that buttress and at once the personality is threatened with dissolution. Now that I actually stood in the house of Victor Frankenstein, I felt myself no more than a character in a fantastic film. It was not a displeasing sensation.

The furniture was light and cheerful. I could hear voices somewhere as I looked around, studying the portraits, examining the marquetry of the chairs and tables, all of which were ranged formally about the walls. A peculiar light seemed shed over everything, by dint of it being *that* house and no other!

I crossed to the window to look more closely at a portrait of Victor's mother. Long casement windows were open into a side garden laid with neat, symmetrical paths. I heard a woman's voice somewhere above me say sharply, 'Please do not mention the subject again!'

I had no scruples about eavesdropping.

A man's voice replied, 'Elizabeth, dearest Elizabeth, you must have thought of these things fully as much as I! I beg you, let us discuss them! Secrecy will be the undoing of the Frankensteins!'

'Henry, I cannot let you say a word against Victor. Silence must be our policy! You are his dearest friend, and must act accordingly.'

A tantalizing snatch of conversation!

Peeping cautiously, I could see that there was a balcony overlooking the garden. It belonged to a room on the first floor, where possibly Elizabeth had her own sitting-room. That it was she, and talking to Henry Clerval, I now had no doubt.

He said, 'I've told you how secretive Victor was in Ingoldstadt. At first, I thought he was mentally deranged. And then those months of what he chose to call nervous fever ... He kept babbling then about some fiend that had taken possession of him. He seemed to get over it, but he behaved in the same alarming manner in court this morning. As an old friend – as more than friend – I beg you not to contemplate marriage with him—'

'Henry, you must say no more or we shall quarrel! You know Victor and I are to be married. I admit Victor is evasive at times, but we have known one another since early childhood, we are as close as brother and sister—'

She checked what she was saying and then went on in an altered tone. 'Victor is a scientist. We must respect his moods of abstraction.' She was going on to add something more, when a cold voice behind me said, 'What may you be after?'

I turned. It was a bad moment.

Ernest Frankenstein stood there. The anger on his brow made him look uncommonly like a younger version of his brother. He was dressed all in black.

'I am being kept waiting with a message for Miss Lavenza.'

'I see you put your waiting to good use. Who are you?'

'My name, sir, since you inquire so civilly, is Bodenland. I come with word from Mr Victor Frankenstein. He is your brother, is he not?'

'Didn't I see you in court this morning?'

'Whom did you not see in court this morning?'

'Give me the message. I will deliver it to my cousin.'

I hesitated. 'I would prefer to deliver it direct.'

As he put out his hand, Elizabeth entered behind him. Perhaps she had heard our voices and used them as an excuse to break away from Henry Clerval.

Her entry gave me the chance to ignore Ernest and present her with Victor's note myself, which I did. As she read it, I was able to study her.

She was small, delicately made, and yet not fragile. Her hair was the most beautiful thing about her. True, her face was perfect of feature, but I thought I saw a coldness there, a pinched look about the mouth, which a younger man might have missed.

She read the note without changing her expression.

'Thank you,' she said. I was dismissed in the phrase. She looked haughtily at me, waiting for me to leave. I gazed at her, thinking that if she had appeared gentler I might have ventured to say something to her on Victor's behalf. As it was, I nodded and made for the door; she looked the sort of woman who won protracted lawsuits.

I went back to the car.

Whatever the time was, it was later than I wished. I still hoped to aid Justine – or rather to correct the course of justice, feeling, in some vague and entirely unwarrantable way, that I was more civilized than these Genevese, having a two-century evolutionary lead over them!

My diversion with the Frankensteins had gained me nothing. Or perhaps it had. Understanding. I certainly understood more about the explosive nature of Frankenstein's situation; hell hath no fury like a reformer who wishes to remake the world and finds the world prefers its irredeemable self. And his complex emotional relationship with Elizabeth, which I had but glimpsed, made the situation that much more precarious.

These matters rolled round and round my brain, like a thunderstorm, like clothes in a tumble-drier. As I drove along the edge of the lake eastwards, I was hardly conscious of the beautiful and placid scenery. A steady rain began to fall. Perhaps it prevented me from noting how rapidly the season seemed to have advanced. The trees were now heavy with dark green foliage. The corn was already ripening and the vines in full leaf, with bunches of grapes hanging thickly.

My own world was forgotten. It had been displaced by my new personality, by what I believe I called earlier my superior self. The fact was that all sorts of strange gear-shifts were taking place within my psyche, and I was eaten up by the morbid drama of Frankenstein. Once more I tried to recall what was to happen, as recounted in Mary Shelley's book, but what little returned was too vague to be of use.

Certainly Frankenstein had gone away to study – to Ingold-stadt, I now knew – and there spent some years researching into the nature of life. Eventually he had built a new being from dismembered corpses, and had re-animated it. How he had overcome all the complex problems of graft-rejection, septicaemia, and so on – not to mention the central problem of bestowing life – was beyond me, although I took it that fortune had favoured his researches. He had then been horrified by what he had done, and had turned against the creature to which he stood as God stood to Adam – that sounded like the baffled reformer again to me! In the end (or in the present future) the creature had overcome him. Or had he overcome it? Anyhow, something dreadful in the way of retribution had occurred, in the nature of things.

In the nature of things? Why should something dreadful come of good intentions?

It seemed an immensely important question, and not only when applied to Frankenstein. Frankenstein was no Faust, exchanging his immortal soul for power. Frankenstein wanted only knowledge – was, if you like, only doing a bit of research. He wanted to put the world to rights. He wanted a few answers to a few riddles.

That made him more like Oedipus than Faust. Oedipus was the world's first scientist. Then Frankenstein was the first R. & D. man. Oedipus had received a lot of dusty answers to his researches too.

I broke off that silly line of thought and retraced my mental steps.

Whatever previous generations made of it, Mary Shelley's *Frankenstein* was regarded by the twenty-first century as the first novel of the Scientific Revolution and, incidentally, as the first novel of science-fiction. Her novel had remained relevant over two centuries simply because Frankenstein was the archetype of the scientist whose research, pursued in the sacred name of increasing knowlege, takes on a life of its own and causes untold misery before being brought under control.

How many of the ills of the modern world were not due precisely to Frankenstein's folly! And that included the most overwhelming problem of all, a world too full of people. That had led to the war, and to untold misery before that, for several generations. And what had caused the overpopulation?

Why, basically, those purely benevolent intentions of medical gentlemen who had introduced and applied theories of hygiene, of infection, of vaccination, and of innoculation, thereby managing to reduce the appalling infant mortality rate!

Was there some immutable cosmic law which decreed that man's good intentions should always thunder back about his head, like slates from a roof?

My dim recollection was that there was discussion of such questions in Mary Shelley's novel. I needed desperately to get hold of a copy of the book. But when had it first been published? I could not recall. Was it a mid-Victorian novel?

There were some fragments of my education in English Literature which did return to me. And that was why I drove eastwards along Lake Geneva. I thought I had a good idea of where at least one copy of the novel would certainly be.

When I saw the next *auberge* coming up, I drew in to the side of the road, put on my raincoat, and walked along to it. I should mention that I had bought a few items of clothing that morning, before the trial began. I no longer looked quite such a time-traveller. (For most of the time, I had forgotten, was unable to remember, my previous existence!)

I was ravenously hungry. At the *auberge*, they set before me a beautiful soup with dumplings in it, followed by a great white sausage on a small alp of potato and onion-rings. This I washed down with lager from a great stein as monumentally carved as the Parthenon.

As I picked my teeth and smiled to myself, I glanced at the newspaper which had been placed, furled on its stick, beside my plate. My smile sank under the horizon. The paper was dated Monday, 26th August, 1816!

But this was May ... At first, my mind could not adjust to the missing three months, so that I sat stupidly with the paper in my hands, staring at it. Then I commenced a tremulous search through its pages, almost as if I expected to find details of a timeslip between Geneva and where I now was.

The name of Frankenstein caught my eye. And there next to it stood Justine's name. I read a short news item in which it was announced that Justine had been hanged the previous Saturday, the 24th, after several postponements of the event.

She had been granted absolution of her sins, but had died protesting her innocence to the last. But – in my yesterday, Justine had still been alive. Where had June and July gone? How did August get there?

Losing three months is a far nastier experience than being jolted back two centuries. Centuries are cold impersonal things. Months are things you live with. And three of them had just been whipped from under me. I paid my bill in very thoughtful fashion, and with a trembling hand.

When I stood at the doorway, hesitating to dash into the pouring rain, I could see that the landscape had moved with the date. Two men who had come in to quaff down great glasses of *cidre* were now returning to their scythes in a field opposite, to join a line of sodden reapers there. The grapes that hung over mine host's door were turning a dusky shade as the juice ripened in their skins. August was here.

The *auberge* owner joined me at the door and stared with contempt at the sky. 'I take it you're a foreigner, sir? This is the worst summer as we've had in these parts for a century, they do say.'

'Is that so?'

'Yes, indeed it is. The worst summer in living memory. No doubt but the discharging of all the cannon and musketry at the Field of Waterloo caused an injury to the normal temperament of the sky.'

'Rain or no rain, I must get on my way. Can you tell me of an English poet staying in these parts?'

He grinned broadly at me.

'Bless you, sir, I can tell you of *two* English poets! England must have as many poets as soldiers, so liberally does she scatter them hereabouts. They're staying not three leagues from this village.'

'Two of them! Do you know their names?'

'Why, sir, one's the great Lord Byron, probably the most famous poet in the world, after Johann Schlitzberger – and a smarter dresser than Johann Schlitzberger he is, as well.'

'The other English poet?'

'He's not famous.'

'Shelley, is it?'

'Yes, I believe that's the name. He's got a couple of women with him. They're down along the road by the lake's edge. You can't miss them. Ask for the Villa Diodati.'

I thanked him and hurried into the rain. What excitement was leaping inside me!

7

The rain had stopped. Cloud lay thick across the lake, hiding the mountain peaks beyond. I stood under trees, surveying the stone walls and vines of the Villa Diodati. My superior self was working out a way to approach and make myself known.

Suppose I introduced myself to Shelley and Byron as a fellow-traveller. How much better if I could have introduced myself as a fellow poet! But in 1816 there were no American poets whose names I could recall. Memory suggested that both Byron and Shelley had a taste for the morbid; no doubt they would enjoy meeting Edgar Allan Poe – yet Poe would be only a child still, somewhere across a very wide Atlantic.

Social niceties were difficult to conduct across two hundred years. The fact that Lord Byron was probably the most famous poet in Europe at this time, even including Johann Schlitzberger, was not going to make things easier.

As I prowled about outside the garden wall, it came on me with a start that a young man was regarding me over the barrel of a pistol. I stopped still in my tracks.

He was a handsome young guy with a head of well-oiled reddish hair. He wore a green jacket, grey trousers, and high calf boots, and had a bold air about him.

'I'd be obliged if you would cease to point that antique at me!' I said.

'Why so? The tourist-shooting season opened today. I've bagged three already. You have only to come close enough to my hide and I let fly. I'm one of the best marksmen in Europe, and you are possibly the biggest grouse in Europe.' But he lowered his pistol and came forward two paces.

'Thank you. It would be embarrassing to be shot before we were introduced.'

He was still not looking particularly friendly. 'Then be off into the undergrowth, my feathered friend. It makes me feel more than somewhat persecuted to have items of the British public lurking about my property – particularly when most of them haven't read two lines of my verse together.'

I noted that he pronounced it in eighteenth-century fashion: 'm' verse'.

Taking the binoculars from round my neck, I proffered them, saying, 'You observe how amateur my lurking was – not only did I not conceal myself, but I did not use my chief lurking weapon. Have you ever seen the like of these, sir?'

He tucked the gun into the top of his trousers. That was a good sign. Then he took the binoculars and peered at me through them.

Clicking his tongue in approval, he swerved to take in the lake.

'Let's see if Doctor Polly is up to anything he shouldn't be with our young Mistress Mary!'

I saw him focus on a boat which lay almost stationary beneath its single sail, fairly close to shore. But I wanted to take him in while his eyes were off me. Being so close to Lord Byron was somewhat like being close to big game – a lion encountered at the foot of Kilimanjaro. Although not a tall man, he had considerable stature. His shoulders were broad, his face handsome; you could see his genius in his eyes and lips. Only his skin, as I inspected him from fairly close quarters, was pallid and blotchy. I saw that there were grey hairs among his auburn locks.

He studied the sailing boat for a while, smiling to himself.

Then he chuckled. 'Tasso keeps them apart, though their fingers meet on the pillows of his pastoral. The triumph of learning over concupiscence! Polly itches for her, but they continue to construe. Red blood is nothing before a blue stocking!'

I could make out two figures in the boat, one male, one female.

I heard my own voice from a remote distance ask, 'Do you refer to Mary Shelley, sir?'

Byron looked quizzically at me, holding the glasses out but

just beyond my grasp. 'Mary Shelley? No, sir, I refer to Mary Wollstonecraft Godwin. She is Shelley's mistress, not his wife. I thought that much was common knowledge. What d'you take 'em for, a pair of Christians? Though neither Shelley nor she are *pagans*, that's certain! Even now, Mary improves her mind at the expense of my doctor's body.'

This news, combined with his presence, caused me some confusion. I could only say, stupidly, 'I believed Shelley and Mary were married.'

He withdrew the glasses again from my reach. 'Mrs Shelley is left behind in London – the only proper treatment for wives, apart from the horse-whip. Mind you, our fair student of Tasso may – *may* succeed...' He laughed. 'There is a tide in the affairs of women which, taken at the flood, leads God knows where...'

The topic suddenly lost interest for him. Handing the glasses back to me, he said of them, with a haughty touch, 'They're well enough. I just wish they spied out something more entertaining than water and doctors. Well, sir, since I presume you know my name, perhaps you would be obliging enough to tell me yours – and your business here.'

'My name is Joseph Bodenland, Lord Byron, and I am from Texas, in America, the Lone Star State. As for my business – well, it is of a private nature, and has to do with Mrs – I mean, with Mary Godwin.'

He smiled. 'I had observed that you were not a damned Englisher. As long as you are not from London, Mr Bodenland, like all the rest of the tedious world – and as long as your business is not with me – and mercifully private, to boot – perhaps you will honour me by joining me in a glass of claret. We can always shoot each other later, if needs be.'

'I hope not, as long as the rain holds off.'

'You will find, if you are long here, that, in this terrible spot, Mr Bodenland, the rain holds *up*, but seldom *off*. Every day contains more weather than a week in Scotland, and weeks in Scotland can drag on for centuries, believe me! Come!'

As if in support of this statement, rain began to fall heavily. 'The sky squelches like a grouse-moor! Let's get in!' he said, limping rapidly ahead of me.

We went into his villa, I in sheer delight and excitement and,

I think, he in some relief at having someone new to talk to. What a spellbinder he was! We sat and drank before a smouldering fire while he conversed. I have tried to convey a pale memory of our meeting, but further than that I cannot go. The range of his talk was beyond me – even when not particularly profound, it was salted with allusions, and the connections he drew between things I had hitherto regarded as unconnected were startling. Then, though he boasted of this and that, it was with an underlying modesty which often spilled over into self-mockery. I was at a temporal disadvantage, for some things to which he made reference were unknown to me.

At least I gathered a few facts, which drifted down like leaves amid the mellow August of his talk. He lived in the Villa Diodati with his doctor, 'Polly', the Italian, Polidori, and his retinue. The Shelley menage was established close by – 'Just a grape's stamp across the vineyard,' as he put it – in a property called Campagne Chapuis: the Villa Chapuis, as I was later to hear it called, more grandly. 'My fellow reprobate and exile' (that was how he designated Shelley) was established with two young women, Mary Godwin and her half-sister, Claire Claremont. Byron raised both his eyebrow and his glass when referring to Claire Claremont.

Prompted by his remark, I recalled that Byron was now in exile. There had been a scandal in London – but scandals gathered as naturally round Byron as clouds round Mont Blanc. He had left England in disgust.

Beneath his glass lay a sheet of paper, sopping up wine. I thought to myself, if I could only get that back to 2020, how much would it be worth! And I asked him if he found his present abode conducive to the writing of poetry.

'This is my present abode,' he said, tapping his head. 'How much longer I shall stay in it and not go out of it, who knows! There seems to be some poetry rattling about in there, rather as air rattles about in the bowels, but to get it out with a proper report – that's the trick! The great John Milton, that blind justifier of God to Man, stayed under this very roof once. Look what it did to him – "Paradise Regained"! The greatest error in English letters, always excluding the birth of Southey. But I have news today that Southey is sick. Tell me something that cheered you recently, Mr Bodenland. We don't have to talk literature, y'know – I'd as leave hear news of America, parts of which still linger in the Carboniferous Age, I understand.'

As I was about to open my mouth like a fish, the outer door swung open and in bounced two hounds, followed by a slender young man shaking raindrops from his head. He scattered drops about from a blue cap he carried, while the dogs sent flurries of water everywhere. In the half-hour I had spent with Lord Byron, I had forgotten that it was again raining steadily.

Byron jumped up with a roar and offered the newcomer a plaid rug on which to dry his hair. The roar made the dogs scatter, barking, and a manservant to appear. The servant banished the dogs and threw logs into the great tiled stove before which we had been sitting.

It was plain how pleased the two men were to see one another. The patter that passed between them spoke of an easy familiarity, and was so fast and allusive that I could hardly follow it.

'I seem to have a veritable Serpentine in my locks,' said the newcomer, still shedding water and laughing wildly.

'Did I not say last night that you were serpent-licked, and Mary agreed? Now you are serpent-locked!'

'Then forgive me while I discharge my serpentine!' – he said while towelling vigorously.

'I'll do my duty by a yet older form. Um – "Ambo florentes aetatibus, Arcades ambo . . ."'

'Capital! And it's a motto that would serve for us both, Albé, even if our Arcadia is liable to flood!'

Byron had his glass in his hand. In the excitement, the sheet of paper that had lain beneath the glass fluttered to the floor. I picked it up. My action recalled my presence to him. Taking my arm as if in apology for a moment's neglect, Byron said, 'My dear Bodenland, you must be acquainted with my fellow reprobate and exile.' So I was introduced to Percy Bysshe Shelley.

Yes, Byron introduced me to Shelley. From that moment on, my severance with the old modes of reality was complete.

The younger man was immediately all confusion, like a girl. He was habited youthfully, in black jacket and trousers, over which he had a dripping cape. The blue cap he tossed to the floor in order to grasp my hand. He gave me a dazzling smile. Shelley was all electricity where Byron was all beef – if I can say that without implying lack of admiration for Byron. He was taller than Byron, but stooped slightly, whereas Byron's demeanour was almost soldierly at times. He was spotty, boney, beardless, but absolutely animated.

'How d'you do, Mr Bodenland, you are in time to listen to a little revision!' He pulled a paper from his pocket and began to read a poem, assuming a somewhat falsetto voice.

'Some say that gleams of a remoter world
Visit the soul in sleep – that death's a slumber,
And that its shapes the busy thoughts outnumber
Of those who wake and live! I look on high—'

Byron clapped his hands to interrupt. 'Sorry, I disagree with those sentiments! Hark to my immortal answer—

'When Time, or soon or late, shall bring
The dreamless sleep that lulls the dead—
Then your remoter worlds, old thing,
Will lie extinguished in your head!

'Forgive my coarse and characteristic interruption! But don't work the poet business so hard. I don't need convincing! Either you are a worse poet than I, in which case I'm bored – or you're better, when I'm jealous!'

'I compete only with myself, Albé, not with you,' Shelley said. But he tucked his manuscript away with a good grace. Albé was the nickname they had for Byron.

'That game's too easy for you! You always excel yourself,' Byron said kindly, as if anxious that he might have hurt Shelley's feelings. 'Come on, have some wine, and there's laudanum on the chimney-piece if you need it. Mr Bodenland was about to tell me of some tremendous thing that cheered him recently!'

Shelley sat close, pushing away the wine, and looked into my face. 'Is that indeed so? Did you see a ray of sunshine or something like that?'

Glad of the diversion, I said, 'Someone told me today that the bad weather was caused by all the cannon-balls discharged on the Field of Waterloo last year.'

Shelley burst into laughter. 'I hope you have something more tremendous than *that* to tell us.'

Put on my mettle, I told them as simply as I could of how Tony, Poll, and Doreen had made their 'Feast', burying their doll (I substituted doll for scouter) and covering the mound with flowers; and how, at the end, as a simple token of courtesy or affection, Tony had presented his penis for Doreen's pleasure.

Although Shelley smiled only faintly, Byron roared with laughter and said, 'Let me tell you of an inscription I once saw scrawled on the wall of a low jakes in Chelsea. It said, "The *cazzo* is our ultimate weapon against humanity"! Though the Italian word was not employed, come to think of it. Can you recall a graffito more charged with knowledge?'

'And maybe self-hatred, too,' I ventured, when I saw Shelley was silent.

'And below it another hand had scribbled a codicil: "And the vagina our last ditch defence"! Your noble savage of the slums is nothing if not a realist, eh, Shelley?'

'I liked the tale of the Feast,' Shelley said to me. 'Perhaps you will tell it to Mary when she comes over, without adding the – unimproving tailpiece.' His gentle manner of saying it robbed the remark of any reproof it might otherwise have carried.

'I'll be delighted to meet her.'

'She'll be here in an hour or so, when she has dried off from her boat trip with Polidori. And when she has fed our little William and tucked him into bed.'

That name – little William! – recalled me to more serious things. The sick, chiselled visage of Frankenstein returned before my eyes. I fell silent. The two poets talked together, the dogs slunk back into the room and fought under the window, the fire flickered. The rain fell. The world seemed very small. Only the perspectives of the poets were large: they had a freedom and a joy in speculation – even when the subject of speculation was a gloomy one – which steadied one's faith in human culture. Yet I could see in Shelley some of Victor's nervous mannerisms. Shelley looked like a haunted man. Something in the set of his shoulders suggested that his pursuers were not far behind. Byron slouched back solidly in his chair, but Shelley never kept still.

A servant was summoned. The laudanum bottle was brought out. Byron tipped it gently into his brandy. Shelley consented to having a draught in wine. I took another glass of wine myself.

'Ah, a man can drown in this stuff!' said Byron, appreciatively sipping.

'No, no, you need a whole lake to drown properly,' said Shelley. 'In this stuff you *float*!' He rose and began to dance round the room. The dogs yapped and growled about his heels. He ignored them, but Byron lurched to his feet with a bellow. 'Get those mankey hounds out of my room!'

As the servant was kicking them out, Mary Godwin entered, and I found myself flushing -- partly with the wine, no doubt, but mainly with the agonizing exhilaration of confronting the author of *Frankenstein, or The Modern Prometheus*.

8

To see her standing there! Although my emotions were engaged, or perhaps because they were engaged, a flash of revelation lit my intellect. I perceived that the orthodox view of Time, as gradually established in the Western world, was a mistaken one.

Even to me then, it was strange that such a perception should dawn at that moment, when dogs were barking, wind was blowing in, everyone was making a hubbub, and Mary Shelley stood before me. But I saw that time was much more like the growth of Mary's reputation, devious and ambiguous, than it was like the straight line, moving remorselessly forward, which Western thought has forced it to prefigure.

That straightness of Time, that confining straightness, was one with the Western picture of setting the world to rights. Historically, it was easy to see how it had arisen. The introduction of bells into all the steeples of Christendom had been an early factor in regularizing the habits of the people -- their first lesson in working to the clock. But the greatest advance in regularity was soon about to descend on the world in which I found myself: the introduction of a complex railway system which depended on exact and uniform timing over whole countries, not on the vagaries of a church steeple or a parson's watch. That regularization would reinforce the lesson of the factory siren: that to survive, all must be sacrificed to a formal pattern imposed impersonally on the individual.

The lesson of the factory siren would be heard too in the sciences, leading to the horrible clockwork universe of Laplace and his successors. That image of things would dominate men's notions of space and time for more than a century. Even when nuclear physics brought what might seem less restrictive ideas, those ideas would be refinements on, and not a revolution against, the mechanistic perception of things. Into this strait-jacket of thought, Time had been thrust. It had come to the stage in 2020 when anyone who regarded Time as other than something that could be measured precisely by chronometer was shunned as an eccentric.

Yet – in the coarse sensual world over which science never entirely held sway, Time was always regarded as devious. Popular parlance spoke of Time as a medium wherein one had a certain independence of movement quite at variance with scientific dogma. 'You're living in the past.' 'He's before his time.' 'I'll knock you into the middle of next week.' 'We are years ahead of the competition.'

The poets had always been on the side of the people. For them, and for some neglected novelists, Time would always be a wayward thing, climbing over life like a variegated ivy over some old house. Or like Mary Shelley's reputation, cherished by few, but always there, diversifying.

She went over to Shelley and gave him a book, telling him that Claire Claremont was sitting by little William – 'Will-mouse', she called him – and writing letters home. Shelley started to question her about Tasso's *La Gerusalemme Liberata*, but Byron called her over to him.

'You may give me a kiss, dear Mary, since it is soon to be your birthday.'

She did kiss him, but somewhat dutifully. He patted her and said to me, 'Here you see the advantages of heredity nobly exemplified. This young lady, Mr Bodenland, is the product of the union of two of the great minds of our time, the philosopher, William Godwin, and Mary Wollstonecraft, one of the great philosophical female minds to rank with my friend, Madame de Staël – who lives just across the lake, as you may know. So we have here beauty and wisdom united, to everyone's great advantage!'

'Do not let Lord Byron prejudice you against me, sir,' said Mary, smiling.

She was petite. She was fair and rather birdlike, with brilliant eyes and a small wistful mouth. As with Shelley, she was irresistible when she laughed, for her whole countenance lit up – she gave you her enjoyment. But she was much more still than Shelley, and on the whole very silent, and in her silence was a mournful quality. I could see why Shelley loved her – and why Byron teased her.

One thing struck me about her immediately. She was amazingly young. Later, I saw by a date in a book that she was not yet eighteen. The thought went through my mind, she can't help me! – It must be years yet before she will come to write her masterpiece.

'Mr Bodenland can tell you a story about little children and graves,' Shelley told her. 'It will make your flesh creep!'

'I couldn't tell it again, even for such worthy ends,' I said to her. 'It would bore the rest of the company even more than it did the first time.'

'If you are staying some while, sir, you must tell it me privately,' Mary said, 'since I am setting up shop as a connoisseur of grave stories.'

'Mr Bodenland is a connoisseur of the Swiss weather,' Byron said. 'He believes it was the cannon at Waterloo which caused the clouds such haemorrhage!'

Before I could protest at the misrepresentation, Mary said, 'Oh, no, that's not so at all – that's a very unscientific remark, if you don't mind my saying so, sir! The bad weather universal in the northern hemisphere this year is entirely attributable to a phenomenal volcanic explosion in the southern hemisphere last year! Isn't that interesting? It proves that winds are distributed all over the globe, and that the whole planet enjoys a circulatory system like—'

'Mary, dear, you upset *my* circulatory system when you parade these ideas you pinch from Percy,' Byron said. 'Let the weather get into anything but *not* the claret and the conversation! Now, Shelley, tell me what you were reading when you were skulking in the woods today.'

Shelley put ten long fingers to his chest and then flipped them up at the ceiling. 'I was not in the woods. I was not on Earth. I had fled the planet entirely. I was with Lucian of Samosata, adventuring on the Moon!'

They began a conversation on the advantages of lunar life; Mary stood meekly beside me, listening. Then she said to me, quietly so as not to disturb the talk, 'We shall eat mutton tonight – or Lord Byron and Polidori will, for Percy and I avoid meat. You must join us, if you will. I am just going to see if the cook is attending to the vegetables.' With that she went towards the kitchen.

Mention of Polidori reminds me that the little Italian doctor had entered with Mary. No one had taken any notice of him. Even I forgot to note it. He poured himself some wine and went over to the fire to drink it. Then, evidently annoyed about something, he tramped upstairs to his room.

Now he suddenly reappeared, clad in nothing but a pair of nankeen trousers, rushing down the stairs and levelling a pistol at my head!

'Ho, ho! A stranger in our midst! Hold, *signore*, how did you get into Diodati! Fiend or human, speak or I shoot!'

I jumped up in fright and anger. Shelley too leaped to his feet, shrieking, and knocked his chair over, so that Mary came running back into the room.

Only Byron was unmoved. 'Polly, stop behaving like a demented Tory at Calais! You are the stranger here, the fiend of Diodati. Kindly take yourself back upstairs and shoot yourself very very quietly, depositing your carcass somewhere where it will not annoy us!'

'It's a joke, Albé, isn't it? It's just my Latin temperament, like your Albanian songs, isn't it?' The little doctor looked from one to the other of us, all concern, hoping for support.

'As you well know, Polly, neither Lord Byron nor I have any sense of humour, being British,' said Shelley. 'Kindly desist! You forget how bad my nerves are!'

'I'm so sorry—'

'Dematerialize!' shouted Byron.

As the man fled back upstairs, Byron added, 'Heavens, but the man is stupid!'

Mary said, 'Even the stupid hate being made to look foolish!'

The rain having petered out for a while, we all went out to stare at the sunset, about which the two poets made lurid remarks. Claire Claremont arrived, giggling and nuzzling up to Byron when she could in a manner distinctly unlike her half-sister's. I thought she was a vexing girl, and judged that Byron thought the same; but he was a lot more patient with her than he had been with Polidori.

Nothing pleased me more than to be allowed to take supper with them. They were interested in my opinions but not my circumstances, so that I did not have to invent any tales about my past. Polidori came down to supper and sat next to me without saying anything. He and I were eating heartily when Byron threw down his fork and cried, 'Oh for the horrors of polite society again! At least they know how to treat meat! This is a mockery of mutton!'

'Ah,' said Shelley, looking up from his carrots, 'Lam-poon!'

'That's a very beefy pun for a vegetarian!' said Bryon, laughing with the rest of us.

'In a few generations, all mankind will be vegetarian,' said Shelley, waving a knife through the air. His conversation changed course with his moods. 'Once it is generally realized that the animals are such close kin to us, then meat-eating will be disdained as too near to cannibalism for comfort. Can you imagine what a civilizing effect that will have on the multitude? A hundred years from now, the march of the physical sciences – oh, Albé, you should have talked to old Erasmus Darwin about that subject! He forsaw the time when steam would invade every domain—'

'Just as it invaded this mutton?'

'Steam is the basis of all the present-day improvements. Mind you, it's only the very beginning of a revolutionary improvement in all things. We who have harnessed steam are now harnessing gas as another powerful servant. And we are merely the precursors of generations who will harness the great life-force of electricity!'

'Well, that's pretty good going,' said Byron. 'That's Air, Water, and Fire. What are our enlightened descendants going to do about the fourth element, Earth? Will they find some use for it, other than burying mouldy bodies in it?'

'The Earth will be free to everyone. Don't you see? Mary, you explain! With the elements as slaves, then for the first time in history slavery will be abolished. Human servitude will disappear, for servitors in the form of machines, powered by steam and electricity, will take over. And that means that a day of universal socialism will dawn. For the first time, there will be no masters and inferiors. All will be equal!'

Byron laughed and stared down at his boots. 'I doubt God ever intended that! He gives no sign of it!'

'It's not *God*'s intentions! It's *Man*'s intentions! As long as Man's intentions can be made to be good ... It's Man that has to put Nature right, you know, and not vice versa. We are all responsible for this fabulous world on which we have been born. I see the time coming when the human race will rule as it should rule, as benevolent gardeners, with a great garden in its care. And then perhaps, like the adventurers of Lucian, we can skip to the Moon and cultivate that. And the other planets of the Sun.'

'Don't you think mankind will have to change its basic nature a little before that happens, Percy?' Mary said timidly. Her eyes had rarely left his face, although he was now tramping about the room, gesticulating as he talked.

'His nature *will* be changed by the changes he has already set afoot!' cried Shelley vehemently. 'The old rotten complacent eighteenth-century order is gone for ever – we are marching towards an age, a realm of science, in which goodness will not be trampled underfoot by despair! Everyone will be a voice to be heard!'

'What a Babel that will be! Your vision of the future frightens me,' Byron said. 'What you predict is very well, and good for the intellectual pulses. What's more, I'd love you to lecture to my confounded wife in that fashion and tell her that *her* rotten complacent way of life is over. But I don't aspire to your Promethean vision of man. I see him as a servile little bugger! You spell him with a capital M, as in Murray; to me he is very lower case. You see despair as something that can be rooted out by machines – some sort of a steam-shovel, perhaps. But to me despair is a permanent part of man, induced by that spectre of three-score years and ten. How can physical science change that unpleasant situation?

'The natural order of things, with all its makeshift arrangements, I agree, is to be railed at. Youth, for instance, is something that should be awarded after a rather stiff examination to men of experience, not wasted on mere boys. But *you* would hand over the natural order to be managed by Parliament. Think how much worse that order would be if administered by the Norths and Castlereaghs of tomorrow!'

'What I'm saying, Albé, is that machines will free all men, all the "mute inglorious Miltons" of Gray's poem. And then there will not be room at the head of a reformed social system for duds and vipers like North or Castlereagh. Ability will be able to speak unmuffled, honesty will be respected. Youth will not be shackled, because the distortions of the present order will be abolished, utterly abolished!'

His eyes gleamed. He stood over Byron, searching Byron's face. For all his dilettante airs, I could see that Byron too was absorbed in the theme.

'Is it possible that machinery will banish oppression?' he asked. 'The question is whether machines strengthen the good or the evil in man's nature. So far, the evidence is not encouraging, and I suspect that new knowledge may lead to new oppression. The French Revolution was intended to remedy the natural order, but it changed very little. It certainly did not stop the corruption of power!'

'But that is because the French still insist on having a top and bottom to society. Socialism will change all that! Just remember, it is the present order which is unnatural. We are working towards a more natural order, where inequality is done away with. By the time you and I are old men—'

'I'll have shot myself before that!'

'By the time this century is finished – the whole planet, well, little Willmouse will live to see it, let's hope ... There are entirely new powers hovering in the air, condensing in the future, lurking in the minds of man, which can be summoned as Prospero summoned Ariel!'

'Don't forget he summoned Caliban, too! What happens if these new powers are seized by those in power already -- who, after all, are in the best position to seize them?'

'But that is why we need a new social order, Albé! Then the new power goes to all alike. What do you say to all this, Mr Bodenland?'

Shelley suddenly swung his luminous face towards me, sat quickly down on a chair, sticking out one leg and resting a hand on his thigh, clearly inviting me to hold the floor awhile.

After all, thought I, I was the best qualified of those present to speak on the subject of the future. And what a pleasure to speak to such receptive minds! I glanced at Mary. She was standing by Shelley, listening intently but saying nothing.

'In one major respect, I'm sure you're right,' I said, addressing myself to Shelley. 'The new systems of machines now coming in have great power, and it is a power to change the world. In the cotton towns, you can already see that power-looms are creating a new category of human being, the town labourer. As the machines become more complex, so he will become more of an expert. His experience will become centred on machines; eventually, his kind will become adjuncts of the machine. They will be called "a labour force". In other words, an abstract idea will replace a master-man relationship; but in practice the workings of a labour force may be just as difficult.'

'But there will be equality – the labour force will control itself.'

'No. It will not be freed, because it will generate its own bosses from within. Nor will it be freed by the machines. Instead, a culture will become enslaved by the machines. The second generation of machines will be much more complex than the first, for it will include machines capable of repairing and even reproducing the first generation! Not only will human goodness be unable to operate effectively on such a system: it will become increasingly irrelevant to it. Because the machines in their teeming millions, large and small, will have become symbols of class and prosperity, like horses to Red Indian tribes or slaves to Romans. Their acquisition and maintenance will increasingly occupy human affairs. Creator and created become locked in a life-and-death relationship.'

'I suppose it's possible ... Man may enslave the elements but remain himself a slave.'

'Nor must you imagine that all innovations will be fruitful.

Imagine, for instance, a flying machine which will transport you from London to Geneva.'

'There is a flying machine in Johnson's *Rasselas*.'

'Would you not think that such a machine would greatly open up commerce and cultural relationships between Switzerland and Britain? But suppose instead that the two countries quarrelled because of some misunderstanding – then flying machines would carry weapons of devastation which could blast the two capitals to the ground!'

'Precisely the conclusion that Johnson arrived at,' said Byron.

'Yes, and as pessimistic with as little reason,' said Shelley swiftly. 'Why should Britain and Switzerland fall out?'

'Because the more they become involved in each other's affairs, the more reason they have to fall out. You may quarrel with your neighbour; you are unlikely to quarrel with someone else's neighbour in the next village. And so in other spheres. The greater the complexity of systems, the more danger of something going wrong, and the less chance individual will has of operating on the systems for good. First the systems become impersonal. Then they seem to take on a mind of their own, then they become positively malignant!'

Silence for a moment, while we all gazed meditatively at the floor.

'Then we are heading for a world full of Frankenstein monsters, Mary!' exclaimed Byron, slapping his leg. 'For God's sake, let's take another drink, or shoot the dogs, or call in Claire to dance the fandango, rather than indulge ourselves in this misery! Is not the past of the human race gloomy enough for you, without supping upon the imaginary horrors of its future?'

The mention of Frankenstein stopped me in mid-thought. So was the novel then written? By this slender girl of eighteen! But the slender girl of eighteen was answering Lord Byron.

'Milton's sympathies would be with you, Albé:

'Let no man seek
Henceforth to be foretold what shall befall
Him or his children . . .

'But my feelings are different, if I may state them. They perhaps correspond in some ways to those of our new friend, Mr

65

Bodenland. Our generation must take on the task of thinking about the future, of assuming towards it the responsibility that we assume towards our children. There are changes in the world to which we must not be passive, or we shall be overwhelmed by them, like children by an illness of which they have no comprehension. When knowledge becomes formulated into a science, then it does take on a life of its own, often alien to the human spirit that conceived it.'

'Oh yes,' I said. 'And always the pretence that the innovating spirit is so noble and good! Whereas the cellars of creativity are often stuffed with corpses . . .'

'Don't talk to me about corpses!' cried Shelley, jumping up. 'Who knows but they may be lined up outside that very wall, waiting to flock in on us!' He pointed melodramatically, running a finger along in the air ahead of him, peering with burning eyes as if indeed watching an army of the dead, invisible to the rest of us. 'I know about corpses! As the cycles of the air distribute moisture about the planet, so the legions of the dead march underground to distribute life! Do I sound so optimistic that I'm not always conscious of the short step between swaddling-bands and cerements? Mortality – that's always the stumbling-block! Your Frankenstein was correct in his basic idea, Mary – he sought first to create a race free from the bounds of ordinary human weakness! Would I had been so created! How I would stalk the world!'

He gave a great shriek and rushed from the room.

Byron pulled a funny face at Mary. 'Think yourself lucky he don't eat meat, ma'am, or there's no knowing what he'd be up to!'

'Percy's so ethereal. I fear the world invisible is more visible to him than to the rest of us. I'd better go and calm him down.'

'Mary, dear, one night when I have made a better meal than I did tonight, I plan to go a little berserk, too, in order to have your solace.'

She smiled. 'Oh, Claire will look after *you*, Lord Byron!'

9

That night, I slept in Chapuis! Byron would not have me in the larger house, claiming that the dogs would never tolerate my presence without howling all night. Shelley, ever one to aid society's strays, invited me to his house. So I slept in a little damp attic room which smelt of apples, my head not very far away from the dream-troubled heads of Shelley and his mistress.

Next morning, I was woken by the baby crying. I thought he probably set up a stronger howl than Byron's dogs!

It was a very ill-ordered household, Mary and Claire looking after it between them in a slapdash way. But I was in a bad mood with myself. I had forgotten my quest on the previous day in the pleasure of the poets' company. Within twenty-four hours, Justine would be hanged, and I had not said a word to anyone about it.

Then recollection returned to me. I had been involved in another timeslip, and this was a day in late August. The summer months of June and July had been stolen. My time-scales were wrong. Just possibly, Justine still lived in Geneva; but in Chapuis she was now one with Shelley's dead, marching underground...

As I climbed from my cramped couch, I realized that my hope of helping the girl was also dead.

But there was one thing I could do. I could eradicate Frankenstein's monster. If I could borrow a copy of Mary's book, I could map its route, ambush, and kill it!

What would Frankenstein do then? Would he make a second creature? Should I also anticipate that it was my duty to eradicate, not only the monster, but the author of monsters?

I shelved that problem for a later date.

One thing you see I had already accepted. I had accepted the equal reality of Mary Shelley and her creation, Victor Frankenstein, just as I had accepted the equal reality of Victor and his monster. In my position, there was no difficulty in so doing; for they accepted my reality, and I was as much a mythical creature in their world as they would have been in mine.

As Time was more devious than scientific orthodoxy would have us believe, so was reality still open to question, since Time was one of the terms in its equation.

Neither girl took a great deal of interest in me. Trunks were standing about half-packed, Claire was rushing madly about looking for her bonnet, Mary was trying to comfort Willmouse, who was crying loudly and looked, I thought, rather a little shrivelled thing. Occasionally, I caught glimpses of Shelley through the vines, skipping about in a somewhat girlish manner between the two houses and the little landing stage where their boats were moored; there were a collection of rowing boats and a masted boat with a deck which Claire referred to as 'the schooner'.

The weather was not too bad. A watery sun had come through, and wind was driving the mist away.

'We're all going to sail round to Meillerie while it's fine,' Claire said. 'I shall take my lute. Lord Byron so loves to hear me play!'

It was obvious I was in the way. If they went sailing, there would be no chance to speak privately to Mary; in two days the Shelley party was leaving here, making for Geneva and thence to London. I crept back upstairs to my little room and spoke my account of the previous day's events into my journal.

In my pocket, I felt a folded piece of paper. It was the manuscript of Lord Byron's poem which I had retrieved from the floor on the previous evening. I smoothed it out and read:

I had a dream that was not quite a dream.
The bright sun was extinguished, and the stars
Did rush eternal through the darkling space,
Trackless and rayless, while the frosted earth
Hung blindly rotting in the moonless air.
Morn came and went, and came, bringing no day,
And men forgot their passions in their dread.

Their habitations – lesser things than light—
Were burnt for beacons; cities were consumed,
So men could see once more each other's face.
Forests were set on fire . . .

failing . . . .

The meagre by the meagre were devoured,
For all were starving by degrees; but two
Of an immense necropolis survived . . .

The world was void, the waves were dead, the tides
Were stranded since the moon, their mistress, fled.
One mighty city only . . .

Darkness became the Universe . . .

I sat for a long while, clutching the unfinished poem, gazing beyond it. I cannot say what I saw there.

At last I realized that the voices of the Shelley party had faded long since. My room was on the landward side of Chapuis, so in any case I could not have watched the schooner depart. Emptiness filled me. From the depths of my patchy education, I recalled that Shelley had drowned in a storm on a lake. This lake? This day? How urgently I hoped not!

Folding the poem, I laid it on the table. All was silence, except for the creaking tick of a clock. At length I stirred myself. In melancholy mood, I went downstairs. There sat Mary, by the empty grate!

She was perched on the end of a bench. Beside her was a wooden cradle, from which she had taken her baby. She held the child in her arms, having undone the ribbon of her blouse and put a small breast to his mouth. She was rocking him gently as he fed and gazing in abstraction at the far corner of the room.

When she saw me, she smiled and put a finger to her lips, motioning silence. She made no attempt to conceal her appealing expanse of breast. Uncertain about Regency conventions, I was both embarrassed and charmed, but she gestured that I was to stay.

The baby fell asleep at its feed. The nipple popped wetly from its mouth. She tied up her ribbons and laid William gently in the cradle before saying, 'I think he will sleep now. The poor little mite has the colic, but I have dosed him up with laudanum.'

'I thought you had sailed on the schooner with the others.'

'I stayed because little Willmouse is unwell, and he will have trouble enough when we are on our way back to England. I also stayed because I understand you wished to speak with me.'

'That was very considerate of you!'

'It was not so much consideration as intuition, for something tells me that you visit me with some strange intelligence.'

'Mary – if I may call you that – yes, I have indeed some strange intelligence. But I know you are a girl with a great deal of intuition as well as consideration, and what you say makes my difficult task easier . . .'

I was head and shoulders taller than she, my head knocking against the low rafters. What I could not say was that, as we two stood in the shadowy parlour, I felt considerably within her spell.

The room was almost bare of possessions, apart from their preparations for departure. On the table lay remains of a frugal breakfast; I noticed nothing but bread and tea and some fruit. A German folio lay open at Shelley's place, with a little duodecimo on it. The subdued light made Mary appear pale. Her hair was fair, so that I thought for a moment of the other woman I had met recently, Elizabeth Lavenza. But Elizabeth's presence had been chilling; Mary's presence was of a different quality. Her eyes were grey, her whole expression animated and a little skittish – or so I thought – from the moment she observed me admiring her breast. With me she had none of the shyness she had exhibited in Byron's company the evening before.

Impulsively, I said, 'You spoke little during our talk last night. Yet I know you had much to contribute.'

'It was my place to listen. And I wished to listen. Shelley was not at his best, yet he always talks so beautifully.'

'Yes. He's very optimistic about the future.'

'Perhaps he makes it appear so.'

A silence fell between us. The baby slept by her feet. Large intangible sensations seemed to rise round us. I could hear the clock ticking again, and the tick of my heart.

'Come and sit by the window with me,' she said. 'Tell me what it is you wish to say. Is it something about Shelley? . . . No, it is something touching on our conversation last night. You don't know it, but my hair stood on end when you spoke of the future as you did. You conjured up for me the legions of the unborn, and I found them as grisly a sight as the legions of the dead. Although, like Shelley, I am not a believer in the Christian religion – as no intelligent person can be in our day – I do give strong credence to spirits. Until you enlighten me, and perhaps even after that, I shall regard *you* as some kind of spirit.'

'That might be the best way to look at it! Maybe I can never convince you that I am other than a spirit, for what I have to tell you is this: that I have come from two hundred years in the future to speak to you – to sit here by this window and talk as we talk now!'

I could not resist letting flattery creep into my tone. Seen in the soft green light of the window, speaking with her serious calm air, Mary Shelley was beautiful to behold. There might be a melancholy here, but there was none of Shelley's madness, none of Byron's moodiness. She seemed like a being apart, a very sane but extraordinary young woman, and a slumbering thing in my breast woke and opened to her.

She said, with a half-laugh. 'You must have documents to prove your claim, to show at whatever unlikely temporal frontier-post you came through on your way here!'

'Of course I do, and better than documents. But the document that most interests me is your novel: *Frankenstein, or The Modern Prometheus.*'

'About that, you will have to give me more details,' she said calmly, gazing at my face. 'How you have heard of my story, I do not know, for it lies unfinished upstairs, although I began it in May. Indeed, I may never complete it, now that we have to move back to England to sort out our difficulties there.'

'You will finish it! You will! I know as much. For I come from a time when your novel is generally acknowledged as a masterpiece of literature and prophetic insight, a time when Frankenstein is as familiar a name to the literate as Gulliver or Robinson Crusoe is to you!'

Her eyes were sparkling and her cheeks flushed.

'My story is famous?'

'It is famous, and your name is honoured.'

She put a hand to her forehead.

'Mr Bodenland, Joe – let's go and walk by the water's edge! I need some physical activity to prove I am not dreaming.'

She was shaking. I took her arm as we passed through the door. She closed it and leaned against it, looking up at me in an unconsciously provocative attitude.

'Can it really be as you say, that fame – that vicarious life in another's breath – will be mine in the years to come? And Shelley's? I'm sure *his* fame can never die!'

'Shelley's fame has always been secure, and his name forever linked with Lord Byron's.' I could see that did not particularly please her, so I added, 'But your fame ranks with Shelley's. He is regarded as one of the foremost poets of science, and you as the first novelist of science.'

'Shall I live to write more than one novel, then?'

'Yes, you will.'

'And when shall I die? And dear Shelley? Shall we die young?'

'You will not die before your names are known.'

'And will we marry? You know he pursues other woman, in his ever-questing way.' She was fiddling absently with the ribbons at her bosom.

'You will marry. Your name goes down into the future as Mary Shelley.'

She closed her eyes. Tears welled behind her eyelids and trickled down her cheeks. Her whole frame shook. I put my arms about her, and we remained half-leaning against the sun-blistered door.

Of what followed I cannot tell in detail – I dare not put it into words. For we were seized up into a kind of ritual which seemed afterwards to have its formal cadences like a dance. Still crying, she laughed. She clung to me, and then she ran away; she dashed through the flowers in the long grass, she twirled around a tree and sent lizards scuttling, she skipped along a sandy path. She invited me to pursue. I ran after her, caught her hand.

She laughed and cried. 'I don't believe it!' she said.

She began to talk rapturously, pouring out speculations about the future, all mixed in with details of her life – which she claimed was deeply unhappy, under a permanent cloud because her mother had died giving birth to her.

'But if I am to achieve such merit as wins fame, then my life has not been so unworthy an exchange for hers as I always feared!'

Again she laughed and cried, and I laughed with her. There was a union, a chemical bond, between us, which nature seemed to acknowledge and conspire with, for the wind dropped and the sun blazed forth, and the great hills with their snowy caps shone forth in magnificence. Without conscious intention, I took her in my arms and kissed her.

Her lips were warm and sweet.

She responded before breaking away. Indirectly, she revealed what was in her mind – and mine – by saying, 'You know why we must return to England so soon after finding this peaceful sanctuary? Because our dear Claire is with child by Byron. That was no marriage of true minds! But today is our own, so let's keep thought of them out! Come, my messenger, who brings me such reason for deep happiness, we will swim in the lake. You know Shelley cannot swim? I swim here with Byron because I dread to swim alone, and tolerate all his impudent remarks. The water's deep and cold as a grave here! Do you mind? We will turn our backs to each other, and so be polite while we strip.'

What man would be feeble enough to resist such a suggestion, or to quarrel with such an arrangement? We were at a little secluded cove, with large boulders strewn about, the debris of some long-past hillside. I could see how clear and pure the water was, how full with fish. There were darting birds in the willow tree overhead. Bees buzzed in the clover. And Mary Shelley's lithe figure was revealed by my side.

She entered the water with a small cry at its chill.

Splashing her limbs to get used to the cold, she turned and looked at me with a hint of mischief, as I stood naked staring at her. Our gaze met and became an eternal thing. That is how I see her now, turning to look over a white shoulder, with the placid expanse of lake about her. I ran forward and dashed myself into the water with a skimming dive.

After our swim, we ran back to the little villa, laughing and clutching our clothes. She found me a towel upstairs. I did not use it, nor she hers. Instead, we lay on the bed together, embracing, mouth to mouth. Time and the great day fluttered round our bodies.

There was a moment later when I found a willow leaf stuck to her still-moist haunches. 'I shall keep it, since it comes from enchanted ground!'

I set it carefully on the edition of Sophocles by her bed, intending to retrieve it later.

'Enchanted indeed! You and I are under an enchantment, Joe. We do not exist in the same world! Both of us are spirits, though you kiss my flesh. And we are swallowed up from the world, carried in this room to a glade of an enchanted forest, magnificent and unbounded, where stand groves of pine and walnut and chestnut. Nothing can harm us here. The forests are infinite. They go on to the end of the world and the end of eternity. The sun will never swing away from that casement window, for we have abolished time at a stroke, my dearest spirit! I wonder what it would be like if you were the last man in the world, and I the last woman? Unknown to fame, we would see the whole world turn back into an Eden about us ... But I would be afraid you might die. I'm always so fearful, you know. Only your good news banished my cares for a while. I had a child that died. Flesh is so frail – except yours, Joe! And I fear for Shelley. He's so wild sometimes. You see what a creature of air and light he is, and yet he has his dark side, just like the moon. Oh, my spirit, my other self, make love to me again, if you can! Let your sunlight and my moonlight mingle!'

Ah, Mary, Mary Shelley, how dear you were and are, beyond all women – and yet what was possible then was only possible because we were mere phantoms in the world, or so we saw it, and scarcely less than phantoms to each other. But the solid Swiss world was no phantom, nor would the solar system cease forging steadily through interstellar space: the sun did swing away from our casement, for all that Mary said, for all our forgetting of time, and the baby awoke and cried; so that Mary, giving me a langourous look, dressed herself carelessly and descended the stairs. I remember how her dress lit the stairwell, reflecting on to the wall the sunbeams that fell on it as she descended.

I followed her down. Our movements were like a formal dance, always related to each other. She got William some milk in a ladle from the kitchen. He drank it, she dandled him on her knee; presently his eyes closed and he slept again, so that Mary could return him to his cradle. Then she turned the full beam of her attention on me. Holding each other's hands, we spoke the name that had united us : Frankenstein.

10

This is what she said when I asked her how she came to write the novel.

'It began as a horror story in the mode of Mrs Radcliffe. One evening in Diodati, Polly – Doctor Polidori, whom you saw at his worst last night – brought us a collection of ghostly tales and read the most gory bits aloud to us. It needs very little provocation to start Shelley off on such topics, or Albé either – he particularly enjoys vampire stories. I do no more than listen to them talking. I can't decide whether Albé likes me, or merely puts up with me for Shelley's sake . . .

'Polidori decided that we should have a competition, and each write a macabre tale. The three men began on something, although Shelley has little patience with prose. I alone could not start. I suppose I was too shy.

'Or perhaps I was too ambitious. I was impatient of inventing *little frights*, like Polidori. What I desired was a grand conception, one which would speak to the mysterious fears of our nature. I have always suffered from nightmares, and at first I thought to press one of them into service, believing that dreams speak from some inner truth, and that in their very unlikelihood lies something more plausible to our inner beings than the most prosaic diurnal life.

'But I was finally inspired by the talk between the poets. I am certain that you know and revere the name of Dr Erasmus Darwin in your day. His *Zoonomia* must ever be cherished for its poetic delights as well as its remarkable meditations on the origins of things. Shelley has always acknowledged his debt to the late doctor. He and Byron were discussing Darwin's experiments and speculations on the future, and on the likely possi-

75

bility of revivifying corpses by electric shock treatments, provided mortification had not set in. Byron said that a number of small machines would be used to set each vital organ going at the same time: one machine for the brain, another a heart-machine, another a kidney-machine, and so on. And Shelley then said that one big engine with various outlets of varying capacities according to the needs of each organ might be used. So they went on developing the idea, and I retired to my bed with those notions in my head.

'I had listened to them spellbound, just as I once, as a small girl, hid behind my father's sofa and heard Samuel Coleridge recite his Ancient Mariner's Rime. There was a nightmare awaiting me that night!

'I could see how the notion of raiding charnel houses for the secrets of life had always been present in Shelley's thought; but these horrid machine speculations were new.

'I slept. I dreamed – and in that dream Frankenstein was born. I saw the engine powerfully at work, its wires running to a monstrous figure, about which the scientist flitted in nervous excitement. Presently the figure sat up in its bandages. At that, the scientist who had played God was dismayed with his handiwork, as was God with our general ancestor, Adam, though with less reason. He goes away, rejecting the power he has assumed, hoping the creation will fall back into decay. But that night, when he is asleep, the creature enters his chamber and rips back his curtain – *so!* – so that he wakes up with a start to find its dreadful gaze upon him, and its hand outstretched for his throat!

'I also started out of my sleep, as you may imagine. Next day, I set myself to writing out my dream, as Horace Walpole did with his dream of Otranto. When I showed my few pages to Shelley, he urged me to develop the story at greater length, and to underline the main idea more powerfully.

'That I have been doing, at the same time infusing some of my illustrious father's principles of conduct into the narrative. Indeed, I suppose I owe a great deal to his novel, *Caleb Williams*, which I have read several times with a daughter's care. My poor creature, you see, is not like all the other grim shades who have preceeded him. He has an inner life, and his most telling statement of his ills is embodied in a Godwinian phrase,

"I am malicious because I am miserable".

'Those are some of the effects which prompted me to write. But greater than they is a sort of compulsion which comes on me, so that when I invent I scarcely know what I am inventing. The story seems to possess me. Such power made me uneasy, and that is why I have put the manuscript by for some days.'

She lay back, looking up at the little discoloured ceiling.

'It is a strange feeling, one on which I have known no author remark. Perhaps it stems from a sensation that I am in some way making a prediction of awful catastrophe, and not just telling a story. If you are from the future, then you must tell me honestly, Joe, if such a catastrophe will take place.'

I hesitated before replying.

'You do have true presentiments of doom, Mary. In that way, you are ahead of your age: I come from a civilization long hypnotized by the idea of its Nemesis. But to answer your question. The fame of your novel – when you finish it – will rest in part on its power of allegory. That allegory is complex, but seems mainly concerned with the way in which Frankenstein, standing for science in general, wishes to remould the world for the better, and instead leaves it a worse place than he finds it. Man has power to invent, but not to control. In that respect, the tale of your modern Prometheus is prophetic, but not in any personal way.

'What makes me curious is this. Do you know that there is a real Victor Frankenstein, son of a distinguished Syndic of Geneva?'

She looked very frightened, and clung to me.

'I can't bear it if you alarm me! You know my story is an invention; I have told you so! Besides, I set my tale in the last century and not today, because that is a convention which readers like.'

'Do you know that your characters are alive today, only a few miles down the road in Geneva? You must know, Mary! You must have read the newspapers and seen that the maidservant, Justine, was on trial for murdering – for murdering one of her charges.'

She started to weep, and cry that her life was difficult enough without further complications. I began to comfort her.

What started as an innocent embrace grew more intent, as I held her and kissed her lips, soft with crying.

'Percy accuses me of not being loving enough. Oh, Joe, do you find me so?'

'Oh, Mary, I had to journey two centuries to find such a lover! There never was a love like ours before! Dearest Mary!'

'My dearest Joe!'

And so on. Why do I tear my heart by recalling our words then?

In our restlessness, we walked about the house, talking, touching each other.

'You must not reproach yourself at any time. You know I must go ... Just remember me as a spirit who brought you good news you richly deserved, no more!'

'Oh, much more, very much more! But two centuries ... I am dust to you, Joe, no more than mouldering bones ...'

'Never have you been less than a living spirit.'

We took little William with us into the garden. Mary brought out a rough-and-ready picnic on a cloth and we sat under old apple trees on which the apples were already beginning to glow with ripeness. Great moon-daisies were shedding their yellow petals all round us; a mint grew in the grass which made the air extra sweet. But I had to return to the subject of Frankenstein.

'Something has happened to us, Mary, that enables us to step between worlds. It may not last. That's why I must go. For while I have it in my power, I must put an end to Frankenstein's monster. You have told me that your book is not finished. But to track the creature down, I must have advance information. Tell me what happens after the trial of Justine.'

She bit her lip. 'Why, it is the history of the world. The creature naturally wants a soul-mate. Frankenstein repents some of his harshness and agrees to make one, a female.'

'No, I don't remember that in the book. Are you sure?'

'So I have written. That is as far as I have got.'

'Is this female made? Where? In Geneva?'

She frowned in concentration.

'Frankenstein has to go away to make it.'

'Where does he go?'

'He has to make a journey, as we must ...'

'What do you mean by that? There is a close link between him and you, isn't there?'

'He's just my character. Of course there's an affinity ... But I don't know where he goes, only what his intentions are. And of course his creature follows him.'

We sat in silence, watching William play and listening to the sound of insects.

'You've told me nothing about your future. What books are written? Do people still believe in God? Did socialism come in? Is my father's name still honoured? What do women wear? Has Greece been liberated? What things do people eat?'

'Human nature is the same. If that changes at all, the change is gradual. We have had wars greater than the wars against Napoleon, fought with more terrible weapons and less mercy, and involving most of the nations of the globe. People are still malicious because they are miserable. Women are still fair and men still love them, but there are fashions in love, as in other things. We hope the human race will continue to exist for millions of years, and grow to more understanding but, in the year 2020, the world seems to be falling apart at the seams.'

And I told her about the timeslips, and how I had found myself back in her time.

'Take me to see your car. Then perhaps I may believe I am not dreaming!'

She carried William, and I led her, holding her small hand, back to where the automobile was parked. Unlocking it, I made her climb in, showed her the swivel-gun, the maps, and many other things to hand.

She made no apparent effort to take it in. Instead, she stroked the back of the driving seat.

'This is beautiful material. Is it from some hitherto undiscovered animal, surviving perhaps in the Southern Continent?'

'No, it is plastic, man-made – one of the many tempting gifts of Frankenstein's heirs!'

She laughed. 'You know, Joe, you are my first reader! A pity you don't remember my book a little better! A pity I do not have a copy bound to present you with! How grandly I would inscribe it ... Are you going now?'

I nodded, suddenly almost too full of emotion to speak.

'Mary, come with me! You are a displaced person, I swear!

– Come and be a displaced person with me!'

She held my hand. 'You know I can't leave dear Shelley. He means to mend the world, but he needs me to mend his clothes ... Do you like me, Joe?'

'You know it goes beyond that! I worship and respect your character. And your body. And your works. Everything that is Mary Shelley. You are woman and legend – all things!'

'Except the fictitious character by which I am best known!'

'It stands greatly to your credit that you warned the world about him.'

We kissed and she climbed out on to the track, clutching Willmouse to her neat breast. She was smiling, although there were tears in her grey eyes.

'You must say my farewells to Lord Byron and Shelley. I am ashamed that I have abused their hospitality.'

'Don't spoil things by being conventional, Joe! We have been phantoms out of Time.'

'Oh, dearest Mary ...'

We smiled mutely and hopelessly at each other, and I started the auto rolling, back in the direction of Geneva.

For a long while, I could see her in the rear-view mirror, standing in the dusty road in her long white dress, holding her child and looking after the Felder. Only when she was out of sight and I had turned a corner did I remember that I had left the little willow leaf from her body lying upstairs on her Sophocles.

She would see it when she climbed up to bed that night.

I I

Geneva began to seem almost a familiar place to me, with its thriving waterfront, grand avenues, narrow streets, and busy horse traffic.

I had left my automobile behind a farmer's barn beyond the city walls, and was making my way to Frankenstein's house. I had resolved that I would make an alliance with him, persuading him not to create a female creature and helping him to hunt down and exterminate the creature already at large in the world.

As if that quest were not macabre enough in itself, I went as if under some sort of malediction. For the date was now early in July. So I had ascertained from newspapers. The harvest I had seen gathered a few kilometres away was back on the stalk.

Even allowing for the probability that Time was no non-stop streamliner, faring ever forward at the same speed every day of creation, some fresh interruption of Nature must have occurred to explain its present serpentine course. Two possibilities came to mind. The first was that the time-shock I had suffered was inducing some highly life-like illusions. The second was, that the grave time-ruptures of my own age, produced by the damage done to space-time, were sending their ripples backwards.

This second possibility was the one I preferred, especially since I saw on reflection that such ripples might produce some of the effects of the first possibility. The time-distortions might cause mental illusions in their own right.

One of those illusions was my persistent sensation that my personality was dissolving. Every act I took which would have been impossible in my own age served to disperse the sheet-anchors that held my personality. Embracing Mary Shelley, enjoying her love and her perfumes, had produced the greatest solvent effect so far. It was a strangely anomic creature who strode up to the door of the house of the Frankensteins and rapped for admittance.

Once more, the manservant was there to show me into the drawing-room. Once more, that room was empty. But only for a moment. Pale Elizabeth came in, imperious and dressed in a satin dress, high-waisted and very decolleté, with Henry Clerval at her side. He was as ruddy as she was pale, his manner as indolent as hers was severe and to-the-point.

Clerval was a round-faced man, pleasant of feature, I thought, but his expression was far from friendly. He made no attempt at any civility, and left Elizabeth to do the talking.

She said, 'I cannot imagine why you have returned here, Mr

Bodenland. Do you have any more messages to bring me from Victor Frankenstein?'

'Am I so unwelcome, ma'am? I did you a small service once by delivering a letter. Perhaps it is fortunate for my own sake that I have no further letter now.'

'It is unfortunate for you that you brazenly appear at all.'

'Why should you say that? I had not intended to trouble you on this occasion. Indeed, I may say it was not my wish to see you at all. I hoped to speak to Victor, or at least have a word with his father.'

'The Syndic is indisposed. As for Victor – you probably know his whereabouts better than we do!'

'I have no idea where he is. Isn't he here?'

Clerval now decided it was his turn to be unpleasant. Coming forward accusingly, he said, 'Where is Victor, Bodenland? Nobody's seen him since you delivered that last message. What passed between you on that occasion?'

'I'm answering no question until you answer a few. Why should you be hostile to me? I've done nothing to offend you. I spoke to Victor twice only and had no quarrel with him. You have more reason to wish him harm than I have, isn't that so?'

At that, Clerval came forward angrily and seized my wrist. I struck his arm down and stood ready to hit him again, harder. We glared at each other.

'We've good reason to have our suspicions of you, Bodenland. You are a foreigner with no settled establishment, you did not pay your hotel bill at Sècheron, and you have a horseless cabriolet that smacks of strange powers!'

'None of that is your business, Clerval!'

Elizabeth said, urgently, 'Here they come now, Henry!'

And I had already heard footsteps in the hall.

The door was flung open and two burly men in boots, sturdy breeches, coarse shirts and bicorne hats marched in. One had a pistol in his belt. I doubted not that they were law officers, but did not linger for a second look, being already at the casement windows into the side garden. Clerval I pushed aside.

As I dashed out, Ernest Frankenstein loomed up. They had had the forethought to post him in the garden. He was a slip of a lad. I struck him in the chest and sent him reeling. The delay was enough for Clerval to catch me and seize me from behind. I turned round and caught him a blow in the ribs. He grunted and got an arm round my neck. I brought my heel down on his instep, and then caught his forehead with my knee as he instinctively doubled with pain.

That last was a luxury I should not have allowed myself, for the toughs were on me. They got in each other's way at the window. Ducking under their grasp, I fell into the garden, staggered up, running already, dodging a flying kick from Ernest, and was away down the path.

They had a long, long garden, with a high wall at the end. There was a trellis against it, which I could climb – but quickly enough?

As I flung myself at it, pounding footsteps were behind me. I hauled myself to the top of the wall, looking back as I prepared to jump.

Ernest was almost at my legs, then one tough, then the second, halting on the path, then Clerval and Elizabeth back by the house. The second tough was aiming his little pistol at me, using both hands to steady his aim – he had had sense enough not to fire when running and waste his one shot. He fired even as I jumped.

I fell into a lane. It was not a very high jump. The ball had hit me in the leg. It was not a bad wound, but entirely enough to make me land badly and wrench my ankle.

Staggering up, I leaned against the wall, panting and gasping, wondering how severely I was hit. With one leg bleeding and one crippled, I had no chance. My pursuers swarmed over into the lane and seized me.

In a short while, limping and protesting, I found myself at the local prison, pushed into a filthy stinking room with some two dozen other malefactors.

How bitterly I thought that night of the happiness I had left that morning! How longingly I recalled that other bed, with Sophocles beside it and Mary in it, as I camped out on unsavoury sacks among the dregs of humanity who were my new companions!

By morning, I was covered in bites from a number of loathsome insects who fed better than I did.

However, I was far from despair. After all, I could not be punished for the death of Victor Frankenstein if he was not dead. Nor was I as isolated as might at first appear. For I knew there were English-speaking visitors in Geneva if I could only establish communication with them; they might be induced to take up my cause. And the Shelley party were near at hand – though the fluctuations of the time scale made it hard to determine whether they would recognize my name if they heard it. And there was the great Lord Byron, a powerful name, a man well known to espouse the cause of freedom. Perhaps word could be got to him.

Meanwhile, my first efforts must be to attract attention to myself and have myself removed from this common Bedlam in which I was shut.

In any case, I needed attention. Though my wound from the officer's ball was not much worse than a flesh wound, it hurt me and looked bad. My trousers were caked with blood. Accordingly, without ever rising from my sordid bed, I lay and groaned and babbled, and altogether gave a wonderful impression of a man in extremity.

Since I was one of the first to awaken, my noise was far from popular, and I received a few kicks and blows from my neighbours, in their kindly efforts to speed my recovery. Their ministrations only aided my cries. Eventually, I stood up screaming, and then pitched down and rolled over in an attitude which (I hoped) suggested death.

A warden was called. He turned me over with his foot. I moaned. Another officer was called, and I was carried away, with much clanking of keys, eventually to find myself in a small room, where I was dumped in a negligent way on a table.

A doctor came and examined me; I moaned throughout the inspection.

My wound was probed and bandaged, and then the fool of a medico bled me, evidently under the impression that it would calm a supposed fever.

As they carried away a pannier of my blood, I felt almost as bad as I pretended to be. I was then dragged into a solitary cell, locked in and left.

There I stayed for two days. I was given some repulsive food which, by the end of the second day, I trained myself to eat. It gave me a bowel disorder within the hour.

On the third day, I was marched before a prison officer, who perfunctorily asked me my name and address, and if I would confess to where I had concealed the body of Victor Frankenstein. I protested my innocence. He laughed and said, 'One of our foremost counsellors is hardly likely to have an innocent man imprisoned.' But he was good enough to allow me some writing materials before I was taken back to my cell, formally charged with murder.

12

Letter from Joseph Bodenland to Mary Godwin:

My dear Mary Godwin,
Your novel found many readers of whom you never knew. This letter may never find you. But perhaps my compulsion to write in these circumstances is as strong as yours!

Nothing but disaster has attended me since I left your side. My one solace is that I *was* at your side. That is consolation enough for anything.

My hazy memory of your novel suggests that you were entirely too kind to Victor's betrothed, Elizabeth, and more than entirely too kind to his friend, Henry Clerval. Between them, they have had me imprisoned, on the charge of having murdered Victor.

My release may come any day, since Victor has but to reappear among the living for the accusation to be proved false on all sides. However, you of all people know how erratic are his movements, moved as he is by guilt and persecution. To misquote you: 'He is itinerant because he is miserable.' Can you help me maybe, by discovering his whereabouts, and perhaps persuading him – through a third party if necessary – to return to his home, or to communicate with the prison officials here? He can bear me no malice.

How much time I have had to meditate on what transpired between us. I will pass in silence over my feelings for you, for they can mean little to you at present (though I am in some doubt as to when 'at present' is), though I assure you that what briefly flowered between us one morning is a flower that will not perish, however many mornings remain.

What I will write about is the world situation in which I find myself. I bless you that you are an intellectual girl, like your mother, in an age when such spirits are rare; in my age, they are less rare, but perhaps no more effectual because of their greater numbers, and because they operate in a world where the male principal has prevailed, even over the mentalities of many of your sex. (I'd say all this differently in the language of my time! Would you like to hear it? You are an early ex-ample of Women's Lib, baby, just like your Mom. Your cause will grab more power as time passes, boosted by the media, who always go for a new slant on the sex thing. But most of those fighting girls have sold themselves out to the big oper-ators, and work the male kick themselves, clitoris or no clitoris. End quote.)

I had put Victor down – and your poet too, I have to confess – as a liberal do-gooding trouble-maker. This troublesome wish to improve the world! 'Look where it's got us!' – that was the assumption behind all I said at Diodati the other evening.

It was too easy an assumption. I can see that now, locked in this miserable cell with no particular guarantees that anything good is ever likely to happen to me again. When Justine Moritz was in this prison, the world outside had prejudged her before her trial. Perhaps I am being prejudged in the same way, if my name is even mentioned outside.

But who would there be to speak for me, who would take up my case? In the twentieth and twenty-first centuries, it will be different, at least in the nations of America, Japan, and Western Europe. That stone curtain will not descend which now shuts off the inmates of prison from the free world outside. Among prison inmates, I do not include debtors – but in the future, governments will not be foolish enough to imprison people merely for debt.

How has this small improvement arisen?

(Of course, I use this particular approach to a general question because I have the subject of prison brought to my notice with a vengeance. But I fancy that if I found myself on the field of Waterloo with a foot missing, or in a dentist's chair without benefit of anaesthetic – a future form of laudanum – or faced with a work-situation in which my family were slowly being starved and degraded, then my conclusions might reasonably be the same.)

Between your age and mine, Mary, the great mass of people have become less coarse. Beautiful though your age is, many though the intellects that adorn it, and ugly though my age is, cruel many of its leaders, I believe that the period from which I come is to be preferred to yours in this respect. People have been educated to care more, upon the whole. Their consciences have been cultivated.

We no longer lock up the mentally deranged, although they were locked up until well into the twentieth century; certainly we do not allow them to be paraded for the general amusement of our population. The population would no longer be amused. (How I loved you when you said to Lord Byron, 'Even the stupid hate being made to look foolish!'!)

We no longer hang a man because, in despair for his family, he steals a sheep or a loaf of bread. Indeed we no longer hang men for anything, or kill them by any other method. We long ago ceased to enjoy hanging as a public spectacle. Nor do we imprison children.

Nor do we any longer allow children to become little work-horses for their fathers or for any other man. Child labour was stopped before your century drew to its end. Instead, educational acts were enforced, slowly, step by step, in tune with general opinion on the issue, in accord with the dictum that politics is the art of the possible.

Indeed, the whole emphasis of education has changed. Education, except for the sons of lords, was once directed at fitting a man for a job and, cynics would add, unfitting him for life. Now, with complex machines themselves capable of performing routine jobs, education concentrates to a great extent on equipping young men and women for life, and living better and more creatively. It may have come too late, but it has come.

We no longer allow the old to starve when their usefulness to the community is ended. Pensions for the aged came in at the beginning of the twentieth century. Geriatry is now a subject which is afforded its own ministry in the affairs of government.

We no longer allow the weak or foolish or unfortunate to perish in the gutters of a city slum. Indeed, slums in the old sense have been almost abolished. There is now such a variety of welfare systems as would amaze you and Shelley. If a man loses his job, he receives unemployment benefits. If he falls sick, he receives sickness benefits. There is a public health service which takes care of all illnesses free of charge.

So I could go on. Although in your native country, England, there are in my epoch six times as many people as in 1816, nevertheless, the individual is guaranteed a much better chance to lead a life free from catastrophe and, if catastrophe occurs, a much better chance to be helped to recover.

(Do I make it sound like a paradise, a utopia, a socialist state such as would delight Shelley's and your father's hearts? Well, remember that all this equality has only been achieved in one small part of the globe, and then mainly at the expense of the rest of the globe; and that this inequality, once such a national feature, is now such an international feature that it has led to a bitterly destructive war between rich and poor nations; and remember that that inequality is fed by an ever-hardening racial antagonism which enlightened men regard as the tragedy of our age.)

What accounts for these social improvements across the whole field of human affairs, between your age and mine? Answer: the growth of social conscience in the general mass of people.

How was that growth fostered?

The burden of Frankenstein's song is that man's concern is to set nature to rights. I believe that when his successors were actively engaged in that process, they often made devastating mistakes. Of late, my generation has perforce had to count up the debit column of all those mistakes, and in so doing has forgotten the benefits.

For the gifts of Frankenstein do not include only material things like the seat coverings which you admired in my automobile – or the automobile itself. They include all the intangible welfare gifts I have enumerated – at what I fear you will think is 'some length'! One of the direct results of science and technology has been an increase in production, and a 'spin-off' or yield of such things as anaesthetics, principles of bacteriology and immunology and hygiene, better understanding of health and illness, the provision of machines to do what women and children were earlier forced to do, cheaper paper, vast presses to permit the masses to read, followed by other mass media, much better conditions in homes and factories and cities – and on and on in a never-ending list.

All these advances have been real, even when dogged by the ills of which I told you. And they have brought a change in the nature of people. I'm talking now about the masses, the great submerged part of every nation. In the western democracies, those masses have never again suffered the dire oppression that they suffered in England until almost the 1850s, when sometimes labouring men, particularly in country districts, might never have a fire in their hearths or taste meat all week, and faced death if they trapped a rabbit on the local lord-of-the-manor's land. People have been able to become softer since those ill times, thanks to the great abundance for which technology is directly responsible.

If you kick a child all his schooldays, force him to labour sixteen hours a day seven days a week, yank out his teeth with forceps when they ache, bleed him when he is ill, beat him throughout his apprenticeship, starve him when he falls on bad times, and finally let him die in the workhouse when he ages prematurely, then you have educated a man, in the best way possible, to be *indifferent*. Indifferent to himself and to others.

Between your age and mine, dear Mary, a re-education has taken place. The benefits of a growing scientific spirit have formed an overwhelming force behind that re-education.

Of course, that's not the end of the story. To have an overwhelming force is one thing, to direct it quite another.

And the chief direction has come in your century – in your heroic century! – from poets and novelists. It is your husband-to-be who declares (or will declare, and of course I may misquote) that poets are *mirrors of the tremendous shadows which futurity casts upon the present*, and the unacknowledged legislators of the world. He is absolutely right, save in one particular: he should have specifically included novelists with poets.

But in your present, in 1816, novels are not much regarded. Their great day is to come in the next generation, for the novel becomes the great art form of the nineteenth century, from Los Angeles to New York, from London and Edinburgh to Moscow and Budapest. The novel becomes the flower of humanism.

The names of these directors of change in your country alone are still recalled, novelists who seized on the great scientifico-social changes of their day and moulded a more sensitive appreciation of life to respond to it: Disraeli, Mrs Gaskell, the Brontë sisters, Charles Reade, George Meredith, Thomas Hardy, George Eliot, your friend Peacock, many others. And especially the beloved Charles Dickens, who perhaps did more than any man in his century – including the great legislators and engineers – to awaken a new conscience in his fellow men. Dickens and the others are the great novelists – and every other western country can offer rival names, from Jules Verne to Dostoevski and Tolstoi – who truly mirror the tremendous futurities and shape the hearts of people. And you, my dear Mary, respected though your name is – you are insufficiently regarded as the first of that invaluable breed, preceeding them by at least one whole generation!

Thanks to the work of your moral forces, powered by the social change which always and only emerges through technological innovation, the future from which I come is not entirely uninhabitable. On the one hand, the sterility of machine culture and the terrible isolation often felt by people even in overcrowded cities; on the other hand, a taking for granted of many basic rights and freedoms which in your day have not even been thought of.

How I think of them now! My case can attract no eager newsmen. I can call on no congressman to worry on my behalf. I may expect no mass media to crusade, no millions of strangers to become suddenly familiar with my name and anxious for my cause. I'm stuck in a cell with a reeking bucket, and two hundred years to wait before justice can be done, and be seen to be done. Do you wonder I now see the positive side of the technological revolution?!

If you can summon Victor, as Prospero summoned his unhappy servants, or help me in any other way, then I'll be grateful. But hardly more grateful than I am already, if grateful is an adequate enough word! Meanwhile, I send you these meditations, hoping they may help you to continue your great book.

And with the meditations, less perishable than a willow leaf, My love, JOE BODENLAND

13

Some of the grand sidereal events of the universe are more accessible at night. With humanity forced into the undignified retreat of its collective beds, the processes of Earth come into their own. Or so I have found.

Exactly why it should be so, I do not know. Certainly night is a more solemn period than day, when the withdrawal of the sun's influence enforces a caesura to activity. But I never had any terror of the dark, and was not like Shakespeare's man, 'in the night, imagining some fear, How easy is a bush supposed a bear ...' So my theory is that while we are in Earth's shadow and intended to be dreaming, our minds may be wider open than by day. In other words, some of that subconscious world which has access to us in dreams may seep through under cloak of night, giving us a better apprehension of the dawn of the world, when we were children – or when mankind was in its childhood.

However that may be, I woke before dawn next day and, just by lying alert on my miserable bunk, was able to let my intelligence spread like mist beyond the narrow confines of the prison. My senses took me through the bars that confined me. I was aware of the cold stone outside, the little huddling rooms of the citizens of Geneva, and of the natural features beyond, the great lake and the mountains, whose peaks would already be saluting a day still unperceived in the city. A barnyard cock crowed distantly – that most medieval of sounds.

I knew something was wrong.

Something had woken me. But what?

My senses strained again.

Again the cockerel, its cry a reminder to me – like the little cake that Proust dipped in his tea – that time is a complex thing, stronger than any tide, yet so fragile it can be traversed instantaneously on a familiar sound or smell. Had another timeslip occurred?

There was something wrong! I sat up, huddling my blanket to my chest.

Not so much a sound as a sensation that a whole spectrum of sound was missing. And then I knew! It was snowing!

It was snowing in July!

That was why I held my blanket about me. It was cold whereas the cell had been stiflingly hot when I fell asleep. It was cold that accounted for my sluggishness in detecting what was wrong.

Snow was falling steadily over the prison, over Geneva, in midsummer ... I hauled myself up and peered out of the bars.

My view was limited to sight of a wall, a tower over it, and a small patch of sky. But I saw torches moving, less powerful than lighted matches against the first crack of tarnished gold in the eastern sky. And there was the snow, grey against grey.

Then the sound, very distant, of a bugle.

A faint smell of woodsmoke.

And another sound, more alarming. The sound of water. Perhaps always an alarming noise for a man trapped in a small space.

How long I stood there, trembling with cold and a nameless apprehension, I have no idea. I listened to attendant noises coming on gradually – the scuffles and grunts and curses of men near at hand, a more distant din of shod feet moving at the double, shouted commands. And always that sound of water, growing fast. People were running now, in the corridor outside my cell.

Panic communicates itself without words. I threw myself against the cell door and hammered and shouted, crying to be let out. Then the water hit the prison.

It arrived in a great flood, a shock-wave of water that could be felt and heard. A second's lull, then such a din! Shouts, screams, and the thunder of inundation.

In a moment, a wave must have swept across the prison yard outside. It struck the wall, and a great cascade burst upwards, some of it to come flying through the cell window. The shock started me hammering at my door again. The whole prison was in a confusion of sound, with the echo of slamming doors added to all the rest of the row.

And worse was to come. The water that spurted through my window was a mere splash. More came welling and flooding under the door, so that I suddenly found it all about my ankles. It was icy.

I jumped on to my bunk, still yelling for release. The light filtering in was enough to reveal a darkly gleaming surface of water, turbulent, continually rising. Already it was almost on a level with my straw palliasse.

My cell was on the ground floor – slightly below the level of the ground, in fact, so that the window had afforded me, on occasion, a view of a warder's waist, belt, keys, and truncheon, as he marched by. Now another wave splashed in. As I looked up, I saw that water was beginning to slop in and trickle down the wall. The yard outside must be flooded to a depth of about three feet. In no time, all prisoners on my level would be drowning – the water outside was already almost above our heads.

Now the din from my fellow prisoners multiplied. I was not the only one who had made this uncomfortable observation.

Splashing through the dark flood, I was again throwing myself at the door when a key turned in its great lock and it opened.

Who set me free – warder or prisoner – I have no idea. But there was someone at least in that dreadful place who had a thought for others besides himself.

The passage was a ghastly limbo between death and life, a place where men fought and screamed in semi-darkness to get out, splashing up to their crutches in fast-moving water. And it was a matter of fighting! To lose your foothold was to be trodden down. A man from a cell ahead of mine, a slight figure, was knocked aside by two more powerful men working together. He went down. The crowd poured on, and over him, and he fell beneath the flood.

When I got to the spot, I groped beneath the water to try

and find him and drag him up, but could feel nothing. Strong though my anxiety was to save him, nothing could force me to duck my head voluntarily beneath that stinking spate. Then I found what had happened to him, for there were two unseen steps down. I also missed my footing and went plunging forward, only by luck managing to keep myself upright.

Now the water was chest-high — more than that as we struggled round a corner, to meet a great frothing wave. But a wider corridor joined here, leading to another wing, and then there was a broader flight of steps up, and a rail to grip. It was like climbing a waterfall, but there was a warder at the top, clinging to a railing and yelling to us at the top of his voice to hurry — as if we needed such encouragement.

What a scene in the yard! What filth and terror and tumult! The water was littered with obstacles, and there were painful things below the water to strike oneself on. But the level was lower and the rush of the flood less severe than in more restricted surroundings, so that that insurmountable dread of drowning gradually subsided.

The gates of the prison had been flung open, after which it was up to everyone to save themselves. It was still snowing. At last I was under the shadow of the prison arch, splashing and gasping with other ill-glimpsed men. Then we were out of the prison. I caught a horrifying glimpse of a great sea stretching among the buildings, of people and animals weltering in it, before turning with the rest of the mob in a rush for higher ground.

14

Hours later, resting myself and my battered legs in a shallow cave on a hillside, I returned to something like my senses.

Although it would be mad to claim that I felt happy, my first feeling was one of cheer that I had escaped from prison. Presumably, the time would come, after the crisis was over, when the prison authorities would institute a hunt to recover their prisoners. But that time must remain a few days ahead yet, while everywhere lay in the throes of a natural disaster – the nature of which had yet to be determined – and while the snow still fell as thickly as it did. I would prepare myself for flight later, for I was determined not to be caught again; meanwhile, I needed warmth and food.

In my pockets was a disposable butane lighter. There was no trouble in that respect. All I needed was fuel, and I would have a fire going.

I hobbled out onto the hillside. My left knee throbbed from a wound it had received in my escape, but for the moment I ignored it. Visibility was down to a few yards. I stood in a white wilderness, and perceived that to gather wood for burning in such conditions was not easy.

However, I applied myself. Enduring the descent of great slides of snow on to my back and shoulders, I rooted about the bases of small trees. So I gradually amassed armfuls of small twigs, which I carried back to my cave. My search took me further from base with each load. After four loads, I came across footprints in the snow.

Like Robinson Crusoe on his island, I trembled at the sight. The prints were large and made by strongly fortified boots. So thickly was the snow falling that I knew they could only just have been made, probably within the past five minutes. Somebody was close by me on the hillside.

Looking about, I could see nothing. The snow was like glaucoma. An image of a great figure with obscured face and mighty vigour returned unpleasantly to my mind. But I went on grubbing for wood.

I worked my way – somewhat fearfully, I admit – into a gloomy stand of pines, and there found several fallen branches which I was able to drag back to the cave. They would suffice for a respectable blaze.

The fire burnt up without much trouble. The warmth was welcome, although now I was nervous anew, thinking my fire would attract anything lurking near at hand. I was too anxious to go looking for birds or small animals which, I fancied, might be caught half-frozen in the undergrowth. Instead, I crouched near my hissing flames, nursing my leg and keeping one hand close to a sturdy length of branch.

When the marauder came, I glimpsed him through drifting snow and smoke. No sound – the universal white blanket saw to that. Only silence, as I rose in fear, weapon in hand, to confront him. He seemed to me huge and shaggy, with his breath hanging about his face in the chilly air.

Then I was struck from behind. The blow landed on my shoulder. It had been aimed at my head, but I moved at the last second, prompted by some unclassified intuition of survival. I caught a glimpse of my assailant, of his ragged and ferocious face, as he paused before hurling himself at me. In that instant, I brought up my branch, so that he caught it right in the face.

He fell back, but the other man, the one I had seen first, came running forward. I whirled my branch. He was armed with a stout length of post, which came up and broke my blow. Before I could deliver another, he had grasped my wrist and we were fighting face to face, nearly falling into the fire as we did so.

I glimpsed the other man getting up and tried to break and run. But they had me! I was tripped. I curled up and kicked out wildly at their shins, but I was at their mercy now. They hacked me in the ribs and then proceeded to batter me about the head.

The fight – the very life! – went out of me. Sprawled in the snow and dirt, I lost command of my senses. It was not complete unconsciousness; instead, I drifted in a helpless state, unable to move. In some broken and unhappy way, I was aware that the two villains stopped kicking and beating me. I was aware of their voices but not of what they said. Their words came to me only as a series of hoarse gasping noises. And I was aware that they were doing something with my fire. I was even aware that they were leaving, but the *interpretation* of all their actions only filtered through some while later. It was as if, owing to the punishment I had received, all the close and companionable cells of my brain had been spaced round the frozen world, so that it took half an hour for intelligence to march from one department to the next. My personal space-time was as dislocated as the impersonal one.

At length, I did manage to roll over and sit up. Then, after a further interval, I was able to drag myself into my little cave. I had a flimsy recollection of being afraid of getting drowned; now I had a flimsy suspicion that I might be buried under snow and never rise again to the surface.

It was the cold that forced me to move. I saw then, through the one eye that would open, that my fire was scattered, that only a few wisps of smoke rose here and there. Later, the knowledge filtered through to me that the two ruffians — escaped prisoners like myself, without a doubt — had attacked me solely on account of my fire. To them, it represented infinite riches, well worth committing murder for.

And was it not infinite riches? Unless blindness was setting in, darkness was. I would freeze to death this night unless I had some warmth.

And there was something else. A noise I recognized among the eternal wastes of silence. Recognized? What ancestral thing in me prompted me to know the cry of wolves?

Somehow or other, working on hands and knees, I drew more branches before my little retreat. Somehow or other, I got a flame going again.

There I lay, half-roasted on one side, freezing on the other, in a sort of trance, more abjectly miserable than I can tell. If I died on this hillside, I would not even know where or when the hillside was.

At some point in that dreadful night, the wolves came very close. I feebly pushed more wood on my fire to make a brighter blaze. And at some point I was *visited*.

I was in no fit state to move a muscle. However, I managed to prise my one good eye open. The fire had died down, though several branches still glowed red. Someone stood carelessly among the embers, as if having his flesh charred was the least of his worries. All I could see were feet and legs, and they looked enormous. The legs were clumsily encased in gaiters.

In a feeble effort at self-preservation, I put up one arm to ward off a blow, but the arm fell down as if it would have nothing to do with such an idea. I could see my hand, lying palm upwards and seemingly a great distance from me. Huge scarred hands thrust something into my hand, a voice spoke to me.

Much later, searching my memory, I thought I had heard it say in deep and melancholy tones, 'Here, fellow outcast from society, if thou canst survive this night, draw strength from one who did not!' Or something to that effect – all I recalled incontrovertibly was that old-fashioned construction, 'if thou canst'...

Then the great figure was gone, swallowed as soon as it turned, into the drifting dark. So too my senses went, into their own brand of night.

15

When I woke, I was not dead. I hauled myself into a sitting position and peered about with my one good eye. The fire was out, or all but, and my limbs felt as lifeless. But I knew I could manage to stagger to my feet and find fresh kindling. I felt a little better, and was aware of hunger pangs in my stomach.

Then it was I thought to look about on the ground near me, recalling that strange visit – had it happened? – in the night. A dead hare lay on the trampled ground, its neck twisted. Some-one had brought me food. This was the thing that 'did not survive the night'.

Someone or something had had compassion on me...

My thought processes were still numb, but I got feebly into action, moving more and more strongly as I sought out wood for a fresh fire. The sight of the flames leaping up did much to hearten me. Swinging my arms, I brought a little circulation back into my aching body. I pressed snow against my bruised face, and managed to melt more snow in my mouth to quench my thirst. Eventually, I was strong enough to concentrate on tearing the hare into pieces, impaling the joints on sticks, and thrusting them into the glowing heat of my fire.

How marvellously good they smelt as they seethed, bubbled and cooked! It was the smell as much as the taste which convinced me that I was still Joe Bodenland, and still destined to struggle on among the living.

The snow stopped falling, but it remained intolerably cold. I decided to strike out while I could, and hope to find help and possibly shelter. It was instinct as much as rational decision — thought was still far beyond me. Indeed, the disintegration of my old personality had taken another long step forward. I was now just impersonally a man, striving against the elements.

Moving with no clear sense of direction, I arrived at last at a wooden hut, set in a clearing in the forest which covered that part of the mountain.

The pure white drifts of snow against the door of the hut convinced me that nobody had been that way recently. After clearing away the snow, I managed to enter the hut.

Inside were a few necessities, a large bearskin, a stove, some kindling wood, a chopper, even a very hard garlic sausage hanging from a beam. Luxury indeed! In one corner hung a crucifix, with a Bible lying below it.

I stayed there for three days, until the snow began to melt, dripping in stealthy drops from my little roof. By that time my body was recovering, my damaged eye was seeing again.

Cleaning myself to the best of my ability, I left the hut and set out downhill, in what I hoped was the direction of Geneva. My attempts to look like a normal human being again were evidently not too successful — at one point in my journey, I came on a man crouching over a small brook from which he was trying to drink. Looking up, he saw me, and at once jumped up and ran crying in terror into the bushes!

Now that my thought-processes were working again, I was eager to discover what dreadful catastrophe had overtaken this part of the world. I could only suppose that the collapse of space-time in my own day was slowly spreading outwards from source, like a bloodstain oozing across an old sheet, threatening many deep-seated continuities. The very idea raised an image of a gradual disruption of the whole fabric of history until, at some stage, the rupture would seriously interfere with the creative processes of Earth themselves. And then, perhaps far back in the dim Permian Age, sufficient harm might be done for the further development of life forms to cease.

No doubt that was too gloomy a picture. Possibly the time-slips in my own day were already dying out. Perhaps the damage here was only minor, a last tremor before the fabric of space-time mended again.

Whatever had happened in space, I had reason to believe

that the displacement in time must have been relatively slight. For what had visited me in my weakest hour and provided me with food if not that damned creation of Frankenstein's? And, if it were so, then the drama of retribution was evidently not yet played out. Surely it was no later than the winter of 1817?

On that I should soon be able to check. Meanwhile, one thing at least appeared certain. If I had encountered Frankenstein's creation, then the creator himself could not be far away. To him at least I could turn for assistance. He would be obliged to offer me some aid, knowing I had information to help him in his pursuit of the monster.

Accordingly, I would go to see him first. Taking care to avoid certain members of his household . . .

So the rational mind lays its rational plans. And then I came to a promontory of rock from which I had a view of Geneva, and was shaken.

The city was there, surely enough, but the lake had gone, and so had the Jura beyond it!

Instead of the lake, my gaze rested upon a broken expanse of scrub. Here and there were dotted beggarly trees or thorns and, right in the far distance, something white gleamed – sand or ice; but, for the rest, there was no predominating feature on which an eye could fix. No roads, no villages, not so much as a solitary building, not even an animal. I saw a river-bed, biting deep into the land, but nothing to suggest that a lake had ever been there or that man had ever trod there.

I stood staring for a long while. There must have been another timeslip. But where and *when* had this unattractive slab of terrain arrived from? So dismal was it that I thought first of Byron's prophetic poem of the death of light, and then of the lands that lie north of the line of the Arctic Circle. The displacement looked to be of considerable extent, much larger than the chunk of 2020 which had brought me to 1816, or the chunk of some mysterious medieval land which had arrived earlier on my front doorstep. I could see no limit to the desolation ahead.

For a while, I turned over in my mind the notion that these timeslips affected me alone. I was weary, and my brain was not working effectively. Then I realized that almost everyone in what I had once regarded as my own day was probably in a similar predicament, that the shattering effects of the war had probably distributed most of 2020 back and forward throughout history!

The reflection implied that this tract of wild land might have come from my own time, the epicentre of the disturbance, and so might be instrumental in restoring me to my own day!

So I resumed my descent towards a much-changed Geneva.

The gates of Plainpalais, by now familiar, were wide. Beyond them, everything was chaos. It was mid-morning, and the streets were thronged with people and animals.

The flood had caused tremendous havoc, breaking down many buildings. Though it had gone now, its mark was everywhere, not least in a great dirty universal tide-line it had painted, seven feet above ground level. That mark decorated humble dwellings and proud buildings, churches and statues.

Now the streets were dry again. So the flooding had not been from the lake – which hitherto I had assumed to be the case; maybe it had come from the river whose bed, now dried, I had seen from my eminence on the hillside.

This hypothesis was roughly confirmed by what I saw when I came to the quayside, or what had been the quayside when the lake existed. The level of the new arid ground was several feet above that of the land on which Geneva stood. The river, suddenly materializing, would have poured straight down into the streets, flooding everything, including the prison.

Something had already been done to mend its path of devastation. I saw no bodies, although I did not doubt that many people had drowned. But the damaged houses were pathetic to see, and wreckage was still being pulled from alleyways and lanes.

A few coins remained in my pocket. I spent almost all of them on a visit to a barber and on a meal, after which I felt my humanity returning. About my ruined clothes I felt less concern, for I noticed that the flood had made many people shabby.

There was the Frankenstein house! It was too solidly built to have suffered serious damage. All the same, it bore the dirty tidemark along its façade, and the garden had been very much beaten down. All vegetation was dying, after July had felt the breath of January.

Remembering what had happened to me the last time I entered this unhappy house, remembering too that I was an escaped jailbird, whom most of the Frankenstein menage would not hesitate to give back into custody, I decided that the wisest course was to keep the place under observation and wait until I could be sure to speak to Victor. So I settled myself in a small tavern just down the street. From one of its windows, I could see the Frankenstein gate.

The hours passed and there was no sign of my quarry. A servant came out of the side gate and returned later, but that was all. As I waited, doubts crowded into my mind. Perhaps I should have formed a better plan; perhaps I should have made instead for the Villa Diodati, to see if I could secure any friends and allies there. At least it would have given me the prospect of seeing Mary Shelley again. Her presence had never left me — throughout my worst hours, her pleasant entrances solaced my misery. Just to see her again!

I was only a refugee at present. With Victor's assistance, it might be possible to retrieve my car; I thought also that I could sell him scientific information, and so escape from my destitute condition. Then would be the time to go seeking dear Mary again. So I stuck obstinately to my original plan.

With dusk, I was forced to leave the tavern, and paced up and down the muddy street for warmth. The villa opposite the Frankenstein mansion was deserted. Maybe the family fled after the flood, or maybe they had all been drowned. I climbed into the garden and crouched in the porch, from whence I had a good view of the street.

A dim light came on behind a blind in the Frankenstein mansion. That would be Elizabeth's room.

I sat looking at that light for almost two hours, by which time I was desperate. I decided to break into the house in whose porch I was sheltering, and search for food and clothes.

Some of the panes in the lower windows had been shattered by flood. Putting my hand in one window, I turned the catch and forced open the window. I climbed on to the sill, paused, jumped in.

I was immediately seized. Some foul glutinous thing got me by the legs and ankles. I staggered and slipped in it, falling against a sofa to which I clung. Gasping, I pulled out my lighter and held it above me to look round the room.

The room was silted up with mud, several inches deep in most places and very deep in one corner. All the furniture had been thrown together, tables and sofas and chairs all in one filthy jumble. Nothing remained as it had been, except for some pictures aslant on the wall. When I got up to walk, glass crunched under my feet.

In the hall lay a body. It was half-hidden by mud, so that I trod on its legs before I realized. I peered down and for a moment believed that I had come on Percy Bysshe Shelley. How to account for this impression, I do not know, although the body belonged to a young man of about Shelley's age. Perhaps he had been so fascinated by the sight of the advancing waters that he had delayed his escape too long.

I climbed the stairs. Nothing had been disturbed here – although the air of desertion and my timid light lent the place a sinister aspect. I tried to banish the idea of a drowned Shelley by conjuring up the memory of Mary stepping into Lake Geneva and looking back at me over her shoulder; instead came a more ferocious image – that of a gigantic man leaping towards me: not the best picture to help one through these present circumstances.

Standing on the upper landing, I could hear a faint continuous noise. It was the sound of mud and moisture, the kind of sound which conjures up bare seashores with the tide far out and clear skies overhead. Mastering my fears, I began to open doors.

The young man's room was easy to identify. I went in. The blind was down at the window. An oil lamp stood by the unmade bed. I lit it, turning the wick low.

He had plenty of clothes he would never need again. I cleaned my legs off on his bed covering and selected a pair of rather fancy trousers from his wardrobe. The only shoes which would fit me were a pair of ski-boots. They were dry and strong; I was pleased with them. I also found what I took to be a sporting pistol, with a beautifully engraved silver stock. I pocketed it, although I had no idea of how it worked. More usefully, I found coin and notes on the dressing-table, and pocketed them.

Now I felt ready for anything. I sat back on the bed, trying to decide if I would not confront the Frankenstein household openly. After the catastrophe, they would hardly find it as easy to summon police as they had done before. Thus reasoning, I fell asleep. Such is the soothing effect of property.

16

The glistering sound of mud was still in the house when I woke, sitting up angrily, for I had not intended to sleep. The lamp still burned. I turned it as low as possible and looked round the blind at Frankenstein's house. No light showed there. I had no idea of how long I had slept.

It was time to leave. One lot of housebreaking must be followed by another. I would enter the house opposite, and determine whether Victor was still about or not.

Leaving by a window on the stairs, I was able to avoid the mud that carpeted the ground floor.

At the front gate, I paused. The sound of a horse in harness, of its hoof idly striking a stone! Peering between the uprights of the gate, I saw that the horse stood before Frankenstein's gate harnessed to a phaeton – or so I believe that type of carriage was called; it was open and had four wheels. It may have been the horse that roused me from my sleep.

I got into the street and stood in the shade, waiting to see what happened. In a moment, two figures appeared dimly by the side of the house. A muttered word or two. One disappeared back into the darkness. The other stepped boldly forward, came through the side gate, and climbed into the phaeton. Dark though it was, I had no doubt but that it was Victor Frankenstein; the darkness surrounding his present movements was so characteristic of him.

Directly he was in, he jerked impatiently at the reins, called to the horse, and they were off! I ran across the road and jumped up, clinging to the side of the phaeton. He reached over for a whip in its cup.

'Frankenstein! It is I, Bodenland! You remember me? I must speak to you!'

'You, damn you! I thought it was – well, no matter? What the devil do you want at this hour of night?'

'I mean you no harm. I have to speak to you.' I climbed in beside him. In a fury, he lashed the horse on.

'This is no hour for conversation. I do not wish to be seen here, do you understand me? I will set you down at the West Gate.'

'You never wish to be seen – that's part of your guilt! Because of your elusiveness, I was charged with your murder. Did you know that? They shut me in your filthy prison! Did you know that? Did you make any attempt to get me free?'

I had intended to adopt a more conciliatory approach, but his whole manner made me angry.

'I have my own affairs, Bodenland. Yours mean nothing to me. People murder and get murdered – so they have done since the world began. It's one of the things that must be altered. But I'm too busy to concern myself with your affairs.'

'My affairs are yours, Victor. You will have to accept me. I know – I know about the monster that haunts your life!'

He had been driving tremendously. Now he slackened pace and turned the pallid oval of his face towards me.

'So you hinted when last we met! Don't think I didn't hope that you might be buried in the prison for ever, or hanged for the murder of which you were accused. I have miseries enough ... My life is doomed. I've worked only for the common good, humbly trying to advance knowledge ...'

As in our previous meeting, he had switched rapidly from defiance to a defensive self-pity. We had reached the city gate now. I saw the difference the flood had made. The great doors had been wrenched off their hinges, and anyone could come and go at all hours. We bowled through them, and out into open country. Frankenstein had made no effort to set me down. So I had an insight into his feelings. He desperately needed to talk to me, to have me as a confessor if not to gain my active help, but could not see the way to come to terms with me; his need to accept was in conflict with his wish to reject. Recalling what I had glimpsed of his relationships with both Henry Clerval and Elizabeth, it occurred to me that this conflict probably characterized all his friendships. The reflection spurred me to take a less over-riding line with him.

'Your good intentions do you credit, Victor – and yet you are always in flight!' There were crates with us in the carriage; he was escaping from home again.

'I'm in flight against the evil of the world. I cannot take you where I am going. I must put you down.'

'Please allow me to come. I shall not be shocked, because I already know what you are up to. Can't you see that I would be better off with you than going to Elizabeth and telling her the truth?'

'You're no more than a blackmailer!'

'My role is not a glamorous one. I am forced into it, as you are forced into yours.'

To that he said nothing. It began to snow lightly again, and we had no protection from it. The horse took a side-track which led uphill. It began to labour, so that Victor spoke encouragingly to it. Together, horse and driver conspired to surmount the hill. All I could do was stay silent.

Finally, we bumped to the top. As we pulled through a grove of bedraggled trees, the horse shied violently and stood up on its hind legs, neighing, between the shafts, so that we were tipped backwards.

'Curse you!' cried Frankenstein, striking out with the whip to one side. Then he applied the lash to the horse's flank, and we were off at speed. 'Did you see it? Where *I* am, *it* is! It haunts me!'

'I saw nothing!'

'Inhuman and abhorrent thing! – It was steaming! Even this cold weather cannot quell it. It thrives on anything that man detests.'

Our present track led to a tower. It loomed dimly in the night and snow. Frankenstein jumped down and led the horse, escorting him through the ruins of outer walls until the tower stood above us. I could make out that it was cylindrical. Behind it, a square building had been added, an ugly piece of architecture with only one window, slitted and barred, set close by enormous double doors. On these doors, Frankenstein hammered impatiently, and the echo went rolling away through the night. I found myself looking about for steaming strangers.

The doors opened and a man appeared with a bull's eye lantern.

We made haste inside, horse, carriage, and all. The man closed and barred and bolted the doors behind us.

'Give me a hand with these crates, Yet,' Frankenstein ordered.

The man called Yet was large and solid, built with an ugly, muscular body. His skull, which protruded above a filthy cravat, was so small that the features of his face seemed to more than cover it; he was bald, which added to the grotesque effect. His lips were so thick that they met the end of his nose and so wide that they became lost in his side-whiskers. He said nothing, simply rolling his eyes and dragging Frankenstein's crates from the phaeton. Then he went to unharness the horse.

'You can do that later. Bring the crates up at once, will you?'

Frankenstein went ahead and I followed. Then came Yet, with a case balanced on one shoulder. Without needing to be told, I knew I had reached Frankenstein's secret laboratory!

17

We climbed the tower stairs. They were well-lit. The few windows we passed were blocked up, so as to prevent light escaping. The first floor was full of machines, most noticeably a steam-engine with rocking beam. This powered a number of small engines with gleaming copper coils. It was only later, when I had the chance of a closer look, that I realized these smaller machines were generating electricity for the tower. Steam-driven pistons turned horseshoe magnets which rotated inside the coils, to generate alternating current. Although my history was vague on the point, I believed that Victor was – in this development as elsewhere – some decades ahead of his time.

The floor above contained Victor's living quarters. Here he bid me stay, saying that there was only the laboratory over-head, and that he did not wish me to enter there. While he went ahead to direct Yet, I looked about me.

His quarters were unremarkable. I noted a few handsome items of furniture – a desk and a carved four-poster among a welter of packing-cases and paper. To one side, a kitchen had been improvised, and was partly shielded from the rest of the room with an embroidered curtain, perhaps as a gesture towards the more gentlemanly side of Victor's life. I took the chance to examine one of the electric lights. It was an arc-lamp with carbon electrodes parallel and vertical, the alternating current of course ensuring that the electrodes would wear down equally. The lamp was enclosed in a frosted glass globe to diffuse the light.

Victor's books attracted my attention. There were old vellum-bound folios of Serapion, Cornelius Agrippa and Paracelsus, and many alchemical works. They were by far outnumbered by recent volumes on chemistry, electricity, galvanism, and natural philosophy. Among Continental names I did not know, such as Waldman and Krempe, I was interested to see British ones, including those of Joseph Priestley, represented by his *History of Electricity* of 1767; and Erasmus Darwin, by *The Botanic Garden, Phytologia*, and *The Temple of Nature*. Many books lay open, carelessly scattered about, so that I could see how Frankenstein had scribbled notes in their margins.

I had picked up a box of letters and was glancing at them, when Frankenstein returned from above and caught me. I said, 'You have a considerable library here.'

'My important possessions have been removed to this tower. It is the one place where I can remain private and uninterrupted. You are holding letters from the great Henry Cavendish. Unfortunately, he is dead now, but his knowledge of electricity was great. I wish I had his brain. Why he never troubled to publish his knowledge, I do not know, except that he was an aristocrat, and so perhaps considered it beneath him to publish. We corresponded, and he taught me almost all I know about the conductivity of electricity and its effect on those bodies through which it passes. Cavendish was far ahead of his time.'

I uttered some platitude or other. 'You seem to be ahead of your time, too.'

He dismissed the remark. 'I still correspond with Michael

Faraday. Do you know that name? He visited me here in Geneva in 1814, with Lord and Lady Davy. Lord Humphry Davy was full of remarkable knowledge. For instance, he taught me how to use nitrous oxide for its effect in combating physical pain. I do so. What other man throughout Europe does the same? Even more vital to the quest I am pursuing—'

He drew himself up. 'I am riding my hobby horse. Mr Bodenland, what are we to do with you? Let me make it plain I do not want you or need you here. If you have information to sell, be so good as to state your price, that I may be left in privacy. My work must go ahead.'

'No, that is what must not happen! I am here to warn you that your work must stop. I have certain knowledge that it will lead only to further grief. It has already led to grief, but that is just a beginning.'

His face was pale, his hands were clenched, in the bitter light from the arcs.

'Who are you to act as my conscience? What is this knowledge of the future you bear?'

'Do not think of me as your adversary – he already exists on Earth. I wish merely to aid you, and ask your aid. Since I was imprisoned because of you, it is only in common human benevolence that you should help me now. Tell me first, what happened to the world when I was in prison. Tell me what the date is, and tell me what the new lands are where once Lac Léman was.'

'You don't even know that much?' His manner relaxed, as if he felt he could cope with ignorance, if not defiance. 'This is July still, though you would not judge as much. The temperature dropped as soon as the frigid lands appeared. They surround most of the environs of Geneva. As to what they are, the academics are still arguing about that. They have posted off to Baron Cuvier and Goethe and Dr Buckland and I know not whom else, but to date have received no answer. Indeed, there is a growing suspicion that Paris and Weimar, and a good many other cities, have ceased to exist. The frigid lands, to my way of thinking, provide good support of the Catastrophe Theory of Earth's evolution. Despite Erasmus Darwin—'

'This is July of 1816?'

'Indeed.'

'And if the lake has gone, what of the lake shores eastward? I mean in particular the Villa Diodati, where the poet Milton once stayed? Has it been swallowed by the frigid lands?'

'How should I know? It is of no interest to me. Your questions—'

'Wait! You know of Lord Byron, of course. Do you know of another poet called Percy Shelley?'

'But naturally! A poet of science like Marcus Aurelius, a follower of Darwin, and a better writer than that verse adventurer, Byron. Let me show you how well I know my Shelley!' And he began to quote, dramatically gesturing in the manner of his time.

' "Among the ruined temples there,
Stupendous columns, and wild images
Of more than man, where marble daemons watch
The Zodiac's brazen mystery, and dead men
Hang their mute thoughts on the mute walls around,
He lingered, pouring on memorials
Of the world's youth—".

'Gigantic bones, no doubt, of antediluvian animals. How does it go on? . . .

"And gazed, till meaning on his vacant mind
Flashed like strong inspiration, and he saw
The thrilling secrets of the birth of time.".

'A poetic echo of my own researches! Is that not fine stuff, Bodenland?'

'I can see why it appeals to you. Victor Frankenstein, Shelley's future wife, Mary Godwin, will publish a novel about you, using you as a dire example of the way man becomes isolated from nature when he seeks to control nature. Be warned – desist from your experiments!'

He took my arm and said, in friendly terms, 'Take care what you say, sir.' Yet was just climbing through the room on the spiral stair, bearing the last of the packing cases up to the laboratory. 'There is no need to enlighten my servant as well as me. He will prepare food for us when he comes down, so mind what you say in his presence.'

'I presume he knows of that – that *doppelgänger* of yours outside?'

'He knows there is a daemon in the forest which seeks to destroy me. He knows less of its true nature than you seem to!'

'Isn't that terrible shadow over your life enough to make you understand that you should desist from further experiment?'

'Shelley understood better than you the passionate quest for truth which overrides any other considerations in the heart of those who would open the secrets of nature, whether scientists or poets. My responsibility must be to that truth, not to society, which is corrupt. Moral considerations are the responsibility of others to pontificate on; I can only be concerned with the advancement of knowledge. Did the man who first harnessed the wind in a sail know that his discovery would be perverted into armadas of sailing ships sent out to destroy and conquer? No! How could he foresee that? He had to bestow his new knowledge on mankind; that they might prove unworthy of it is an entirely different question.'

Seeing that Yet returned to the room and went behind the curtain to prepare us the meal Frankenstein had promised, he lowered his voice and continued, 'I bestow my gift of the secret of life upon mankind. They must make of it what they will. If your argument were to prevail, and to have prevailed, then mankind would still be living in primitive ignorance, habited in the skins of animals, for fear of new things.'

The argument he used was still being used in the time from which I came, give or take a little rodomontade. I was sick to counter it, since I saw a glimmer of enjoyment in his eye; he had said it all before, and liked saying it.

'Logic will not sway you, I know. You are in the grip of an obsession. It is useless for me to point out that scientific curiosity by itself is as irresponsible as the curiosity of a child. It amounts to meddling, no more. You have to accept responsibility for the fruits of your actions, in the scientific field as elsewhere. You say you have bestowed your gift of the secret of life on mankind, but in fact you have done nothing of the sort. I happen to know that you have created life through some accident – yes, Victor, an accident, for all your deliberate intent, because understanding of flesh, limb, and organ grafts, of immunology, and a dozen other -ologies, will not come for several generations. Yours is luck, not knowledge. Besides, how have you *bestowed* this gift? In the most beggarly way possible! By keeping the pride of achievement entirely to yourself and letting only the foul consequences of your activities out on the community! Your younger brother William strangled, remember, your excellent servant Justine Moritz wrongly hanged for his death, remember? Are these the gifts you so grandly claim to have bestowed on mankind? If mankind knew to whom it should be grateful, don't you think they would come storming up the hill and burn down your tower with all its foul secrets?'

My speech had touched him! I saw in him again that curious crumbling, a moral crumbling that was evident when he spoke again, almost in a whining tone.

'Who are you to preach at me? You don't have my fears, my burdens! Why do you add to my miseries by haunting me and confronting me with my sins?'

At this juncture, Yet appeared and stood stolidly at Frankenstein's elbow, bearing a tray. Frankenstein took it automatically and dismissed the man with a curt gesture.

As he set plates of cold meat, potato, and onion before us, he said, 'You don't know how I am threatened. My creature, my invention, in whom I instilled the gift of life, escaped from my care. In captivity, he would have caused no pain, would have remained ignorant of his lot. In freedom, he managed to hide away in the wilds and educate himself. Education should only be bestowed on the few. Few are they who can manage to live with ideas. My – my monster, if you will, learnt to talk and even learnt to read. He found a leathern portmanteau containing books. Was that my fault?'

He had recovered his composure, and faced up to me with a chill warmth.

'So it befell that he read Goethe's *The Sorrows of Young Werther* and discovered the nature of love. He read Plutarch's *Lives*, and discovered the nature of human struggle. And, most unfortunately, he read Milton's great poem, *Paradise Lost*, from which he discovered religion. You can imagine how damaging such great books were, casting their spells on a completely untutored mind!'

'Untutored! How can you claim that? Isn't your creature's brain stolen from a corpse that once had life and thought?'

'Pah, nothing's left from the previous existence – only the mere lees and dregs of thought, dreams of past time that the creature does not heed, or not half as much as the figments he has derived from Milton! He now has himself cast in the role of Satan, and I in the role of God Almighty. And he demands that I create for him a mate, a gigantic Eve to give him solace.'

'You must not do it!'

I saw him glance involuntarily upwards, as if in the direction of Heaven or, possibly, the floor above. The latter was more likely; he did not seem to have a great deal of time for God.

'But what a project!' he said. 'To improve on one's first blundering attempts . . .'

'You are mad! Do you want two fiends after you, instead of one? At present, your monster has reason to spare your life. But when you have equipped him with a wife – why, it will be in his interest to kill you!'

He rested his head on his hand with a weary gesture. 'How can you comprehend the difficulties of my situation? Why am I talking to you like this? The creature has uttered the direst of threats – not against my life, which is of little account, but against Elizabeth's. "I will be with you on your wedding night!" That was what he said. If he cannot have a wedding, he will not allow mine. If I will not bring his bride to life, then he will rob my bride of her life.'

Something in my throat almost choked me. He had revealed more of his degraded sensibilities than he knew, in thus equating himself with his travesty of life and Elizabeth with some monster yet uncreated.

I stood up. 'You already have one implacable enemy. In me you will have a second unless you agree that we go tomorrow into the city and lay the entire matter before the syndics. Do you plan to populate the world with monsters?'

'You're being too hasty, Bodenland!'

'Not a moment too hasty! Come, agree! – We go in the morning?'

He sat looking at me, his mouth turned down in a bitter line. Then, abruptly, his gaze lowered, and he began to fiddle with a knife.

'Let's eat without quarrelling,' he said. 'I'll decide after the meal. Look, I'll get us some wine. You'd like to drink some wine.'

His face was shining, maybe from the heat of the lights. He looked more than ever as if stamped out of metal.

There were bottles of red wine on a cabinet, and elegant glasses beside them. Victor snatched up a bottle and two glasses, and took them behind his curtain into the kitchen. 'I'll open this bottle,' he called.

He was some while. When he returned, he carried two brimming glasses.

'Drink, eat! Though civilization crumbles, let those who are civilized remain so to the end! A toast to you, Bodenland!' He raised his glass.

I was overcome by a fit of coughing. Could it be – could it possibly be – that he had poisoned or drugged my wine? The idea seemed too melodramatically absurd, until I recalled that all melodrama has its basis in the lurid facts of earlier generations.

'It's so hot under your lights,' I said. 'Could we not open a window?'

'Nonsense, it's snowing outside. Drink up!'

'But that window over there – I thought I heard a noise at it a moment ago . . .'

That was more effective. He was up and over to it, peering behind the wooden panel that blocked its panes.

'Nothing there. We are far enough above the ground . . . But that fiend is capable of building a ladder . . .' This was muttered apprehensively to himself. He came back and sat down, raising his glass again and staring at me intently.

Now I raised my glass with more confidence, for I had switched it for his. We both drank, staring at each other. I could see the nervous tension in him. So compulsively did he watch me empty my glass that he drained his own in compulsive sympathy.

I let my mouth fall open and set my glass down heavily on the table, allowing my head to fall back against the chair and my eyes to close, in the imitation of unconsciousness.

'Precisely—' he said. 'Precisely—'

He struggled to get up from his chair. His glass fell to the floor, and landed on a rug without breaking. Victor would have fallen too, had I not run round the table and caught him as he staggered. His body was completely limp. His heart still beat, and a dew of sweat lay on his forehead.

When I had stretched him out on the floor, I stood over him. Now what should I do?

My position was not the most comfortable one. Below me was Yet and, even if I bluffed my way past him, the monster lurked outside. In any case, now if ever was my chance to ruin Victor's plans. As Frankenstein's gaze had recently done, my gaze turned up to the ceiling, beyond which lay the laboratory – with all its gruesome secrets now accessible to me!

18

The spiral stair wound upwards, clinging to the rough stone wall of the tower. I hastened up its wormy treads. The door at the top was fortified with extra timbers, and there were newly installed bolts on the door.

I slid back the bolts and pushed the door open.

Beyond was a completely cylindrical room, its beamed ceiling some nine feet high. One arc-lamp burned in the middle of the room, sending a gleam spluttering over the accumulated apparatus of the laboratory. Frankenstein's lights generated a lot of heat. To keep the temperature low, a skylight in the ceiling had been opened a crack; a few flakes of snow drifted about the room before melting.

My interest – my fascinated, horrified interest – was centred on a great bench to one side of the room. A monstrous form lay on it, covered by sheeting. I could see by its outline that it was at least dimly human.

Of the machines clustering about the bench, I gained no clear idea, except that, by the head, a tank of a red liquid stood above it, dripping its contents down a tube which led under the sheet. And there were other tubes and other wires which crept under there, coupled to other tanks and other machines which quivered and laboured as if they also had some dim expectation of life. They did their work to the accompaniment of siphoning and sucking noises.

A terrible fear was on me. The place smelt of preserving fluid and decay, laced with other stenches. I knew I had to approach that silent figure. I had to wreck it and the equipment sustaining it, but my limbs would not propel me forward.

I looked about the place. On the wall hung beautiful diagrams in the manner of Leonardo da Vinci of the musculature of limbs and the action of levers. There were elegant Calcar skeletons from Vesalius, and diagrams of the nervous system, as well as anatomical charts marked in many colours. On shelves to one side stood retorts containing limbs with the flesh still on them, floating in preserving fluid – human limbs, I supposed, but did not attempt to identify them. And there were preserved sexual organs, male and female, some of them unmistakably animal. And a series of foetuses, beginning to decay in their jars. And what I took for a womb, slowly flaking apart with age. And numerous models in coloured waxes, built to imitate the things in the jars. And other models, of bones and organs, made in wood and various metals.

One whole shelf was devoted to the human skull. Some had been sawn laterally, some vertically, to reveal the complex chambers inside. Some had been part-filled with coloured wax. Others were cosmeticized in a strange way, with banked eye-sockets, raised cheekbones, altered brows, modified noses. The effect was of a row of fantastic helmets.

My fear was leaving me, overtaken by curiosity. In particular, I studied for some while a figure chalked on a great blackboard which stood close to the bench bearing the sheeted body.

The chalk figure outlined a human being. There were perfunctory indications of a face; flowing hair, and the more carefully sketched genitals, showed that a female was depicted. Departures from normal human anatomy were marked in red. The diagram represented six extra ribs, thus greatly increasing the lung-cage. The respiratory system had been modified, so that air could be breathed in through the nose, as customary, but out through apertures behind the ears. A magnified detail drew attention to the skin; although I could not understand the symbols appended, it looked as if the idea was that the outer skin should have less sensibility, by the withdrawal of nerves and capilliary blood-vessels from the outer layers of the epidermis – in fact, that a sort of hide should develop over the flesh which would render its owner fairly immune to extremes of temperature. Again, the uro-genital tract had been modified. The vaginal area served purely for purposes of procreation; a sort of vestigial mock-penis was provided on the thigh, from which urine could be expelled. I looked at this detail with some interest, thinking it would probably tell a psychologist a great deal about Victor Frankenstein's thought processes during this period of his engagement.

Perhaps the most unusual feature of the diagram was that it represented the figure as having a twin backbone. This allowed for great strengthening in a traditionally weak region. The pelvis was also fortified, so that greater musculature was allowed in the legs. I thought of that spectral figure I had seen climbing Mont Salève so rapidly, and began to understand the magnitude of Frankenstein's accomplishments and ambitions!

Across one side of the laboratory, a noble four-panelled screen embossed with emblematic figures had been drawn. Skirting the bench with its sheeted figure, I went and looked behind it.

This was – what do I call it? A charnel house? A dissecting room? On a slab and piled into a stone sink were torsos of human beings, one or two of them opened and filleted like pigs' carcasses. And there were legs and knee-sockets and slabs of unidentifiable meat. A slender female torso – headless but with arms – was pinned to the wall; one shoulder had been flayed to reveal a network of muscles.

I looked away at once. It was a gruesome cache of spare parts!

Now I turned to the principal occupant of Frankenstein's laboratory, to that sheeted figure lying on its bench surrounded by snuffling machines. I told myself that this was merely a self-set problem in human engineering. Small wonder that the monster regarded his creator as God Almighty! Until now, I had looked on the legendary Frankenstein as a sort of piece-meal dabbler in cadavers, a small-time crank who haunted crypts and graves for mismatched eyes and hands. My error was the fault of movie-makers and other horror merchants. My dear Mary had had a truer idea when she called Victor 'The Modern Prometheus'.

Even so, the error may have started with Mary. For she had in some fashion, through her perceptive and precognitive powers – which in many ways she shared with Shelley – received Frankenstein's story from the thin air, as far as I could determine. No doubt that story contained many scientific theories which she had had to omit from her tale, being unable to comprehend them. I would have been forced to do the same myself. Only now it was clear to me what an achievement was Victor Frankenstein's, and how strong in him must be the desire to continue his line of research, whatever its consequences. So I stepped forward boldly and pulled the sheets away from what they concealed.

There lay a great female figure, naked except for the pipes and wires that fed or drained her.

Clutching the sheet, letting a great hollow groan escape me, I staggered back across the room. That face! That face, though the hair had been shaven from its head, leaving the skull bald and patterned with livid scars – that face was the face of Justine Moritz. Her eyes, muzzy with death, seemed to be regarding mine.

19

For a space, my heart was almost as still as hers.

Now I saw starkly, for the first time, the villainy and the sheer horror of Frankenstein's researches. The dead are impersonal, and so perhaps it is of no especial moment that they should be disturbed – or so I might once have argued on Victor's behalf. But to press into service, as though it were no more than a compendium of useful organs, the body of a servant, a friend – and a friend, at that, who died for a crime attributable to one's own negligence – well, this moral madness placed him beyond human consideration.

At that moment, the determination came to me to kill Victor Frankenstein as well as his creature.

Yet, while one part of my mind was reaching this decision, while horror and moral indignation were mounting me, another part of my mind was working in an opposite direction.

Despite myself, my regard was still held by the stupendous figure prone before me. The body had been formed from more than one carcass. Skin tones varied, and scars like scarlet ropes ran about the anatomy, so that one was reminded of a butcher's diagram. I could not help seeing that the amendments sketched on the blackboard had been executed; the modified organs were in place. The legs were far from female. They had too much muscle, too much hair, and were tremendously thick at the thigh. The extra ribs had been added, giving an enormous rib-cage, topped by gigantic if flaccid breasts, powerful enough to suckle a whole brood of infant monsters.

My reaction to all this was not one of horror. For Frankenstein's researches I felt horror, yes. But confronted with this unbreathing creature surmounted by that frozen but guiltless female face, I felt only pity. It was pity mainly for the weakness of human flesh, for the sad imperfection of us as a species, for our nakedness, our frail hold on life. To be, to remain human was always a struggle, and the struggle always ultimately rewarded by death. True, the religious believed that death was only physical; but I had never allowed my instinctive religious feelings to come to the surface. Until now.

Victor's plan for this creature's coming resurrection would be a blasphemy. What had been done, in this inspired cobbling together of corpses, was a blasphemy. And to say as much – to think as much – was to admit religion, to admit that life held more than the grave at the end of it, to admit that there was a spirit which transcended the poor imperfect flesh. Flesh without spirit was obscene. Why else should the notion of Frankenstein's monster have affronted the imagination of generations if it was not their intuition of God that was affronted?

To report my inner thoughts at such a moment of crisis must be to vex anyone who listens to this tape. Yet I am impelled to go on.

For the conflict of emotions in me caused me to burst into tears. I fell on my knees and wept, and called aloud to God. I buried my face in my hands and cried with helplessness.

Perhaps one detail I have not mentioned led to this unexpected response in me. On the stool by the side of the female stood a jar with flowers in it, crimson and yellow.

There was another turn to the screw of my misery. For at that moment I thought I saw that all my previous beliefs in progress were built on shifting sand. How often, in my past life, I had claimed that one of the great benefits the nineteenth century had conferred on the West had been science's liberation of thought and feeling from organized religion. Organized religion, indeed! What had we in its place? Organized science! Whereas organized religion was never well organized, and often ran contrary to commercial interests, it had been forced to pay lip service, if not more than that, to the idea that there was a place in the scheme of things for the least among us. But organized science had allied itself with Big Business and Government; it had no interest in the individual – its meat was statistics! It was death to the spirit.

As science had gradually eroded the freedom of time, so it had eroded the freedom of belief. Anything which could not be proven in a laboratory by scientific method – anything, that is to say, which was bigger than science – was ruled out of court. God had long been banished in favour of any number of grotty little sects, clinging to tattered bits of faith; they could be tolerated, since they formed no collective alternative to the consumer society on which organized science depended so heavily.

The Frankenstein mentality had triumphed by my day. Two centuries was all it needed. The head had triumphed over the heart.

Not that I had ever believed in the heart marching ahead alone. That had been as grievous a thing as seeing the head triumph; that had caused the centuries of religious persecutions and wars. But there had been a time, early in the nineteenth century, in Shelley's day, where the head and the heart had stood a chance of marching forward together. Now it had disappeared, even as Mary's Diseased Creation myth had prophesied.

Inevitably, I am elaborating after the event in intellectual terms. What I experienced as I fell on my knees was a metaphor – I saw the technological society into which I had been born as a Frankenstein body from which the spirit was missing.

I wept for the mess of the world.

'Oh, God!' I cried.

There was a sound above me, and I looked upwards.

A great beautiful face stared down at me. For a moment – then the skylight in the beamed roof was flung up, and Frankenstein's Adam came leaping down to stand before me in his wrath!

Until this wretched point in my narrative, I believe I have given a fairly good account of myself. I had acted with some courage and endurance – and even intelligence, I hope – in a situation many men would have found hopeless. Yet here I was, snivelling on my hands and knees. And all I could do at this terrible invasion was to rise and stand mutely, with my hands by my sides, staring up at this tremendous being – whom I now saw clearly for the first time.

In his anger, he was beautiful. I use the word beautiful knowing it to be inaccurate, yet not knowing how else to counteract the myth which has circulated for two centuries that Frankenstein's monster's face was a hideous conglomeration of second-hand features.

It was not so. Perhaps the lie drew its life from a human longing for those chills of horror which are depraved forms of religious awe. And I must admit that Mary Shelley began the rumour; but she had to make her impression on an untutored audience. I can only declare that the face before me had a terrible beauty.

Of course, terror predominated. It was very far from being a human face. It resembled much more one of the helmet faces painted on the skulls in the rack behind me. Evidently, Frankenstein had been unable to create a face that pleased him. But he had given patient thought to the matter, just as he had to the rest of the alien anatomy; and he had ventured on what I can only call an abstraction of the human face.

The eyes were there, glaring down at me from behind high defensive cheekbones, as if through the slits of a visor. The other features, the mouth, the ears, and especially the nose, had been blurred in some fashion by the surgeon's knife. The creature that now stared down at me looked like a machine, lathe-turned.

His skull almost knocked against the beams of the ceiling. He bent, seized my wrist, and dragged me towards him as if I were no more than a doll.

20

'You are forbidden by my Creator to be in here!'

Those were the first words the nameless monster spoke to me. They were delivered quietly, in a deep voice – 'a voice from the grave' was the association the tone aroused. Quiet though the words were, they carried no reassurance. This powerful being need make no special effort to quell me.

The great hand that held me was a mottled blue, crusted and filthy. From its throat, where a carelessly tied scarf failed to conceal deep scars, to its feet, encased in boots that I imagined I recognized, the monster was a monument to grime. It was encrusted in mud and blood and excrement, so that its great-coat was plastered against its trousers. Snow fell to the floor from it and melted. It still steamed slightly, so damp was it. This indifference to its wretched state was a further cause for alarm.

Shaking me slightly – so that my teeth rattled – it said, 'This is no place for you, whoever you may be.'

'You saved my life when I was dying on the hillside.' The words happened to be the first I could enunciate.

'My role is not to spare life but to protect my own. Who am I to be merciful? All men are my enemies, and every living hand is turned against me.'

'You saved my life. You brought me a hare to eat when I was starving to death.'

He – I must cease to refer to him as an *it* – he let go of me, and I managed to remain standing in his dreadful presence.

'You – are – grateful – to – me?'

'You spared my life. I am grateful for that gift, as perhaps you may be.'

He rumbled. 'I have no life while everyone's hand is turned against me. As I am without sanctuary, so I am without gratitude. My Creator gave me life, and the profit of it is I know how to curse; he gave me feeling, and the profit of it is I know how to suffer! I am Fallen! Without his love, his aid, I am Fallen.

' "Why is life given
To be thus wrested from us? Rather why
Obtruded on us thus? Who, if we knew
What we receive, would either not accept
Life offered, or soon beg to lay it down,
Glad to be so dismissed in peace . . ."

'Are not those the words in the great Miltonic book? But, under threat, my Creator has agreed to make me this Eve with whom you interfere, uncovering her nakedness. She will make my misery more tolerable, my slavery only half-slavery, my exile less a banishment. What are you doing in such a place? Why has He allowed you here? What mischief have you done Him?'

'None, none!' – fearing he might go downstairs and find Frankenstein in a state he would possibly mistake for lifeless.

He seized my arm again.

'Nobody is allowed to do Him mischief but me! I am His protector as long as He works on this project! Now, tell me what you have done with Him? Are you the Serpent, to come here like this, filthy and venomous?'

For a moment he turned towards the creature that wore the face of Justine. He stretched out an arm and placed a gnarled hand tenderly on her scarred brow; then he turned back to me.

'We'll see what you have done! Nothing can be hidden from me!'

Dragging me, he strode to the door in two strides, and flung it open. I struggled, but he did not even notice. Without a pause, he moved down the stairs. His movements were rapid and inhuman. I had to run with him, dreading what would come next.

Victor Frankenstein still lay senseless on the carpet below. Someone was with him. His servant Yet was bending over him, and had Victor's head against his knee. He looked up angrily, then yelled with terror, and jumped to his feet. The monster, coming forward, knocked him out of the way with one sweep of an arm as he marched towards the prone figure of his creator. The force of the casual blow was such that Yet was flung back against a bookcase. Books showered about him.

As for me, I was dragged forward at that awful pace, like a toy dog on a lead. The monster bent clumsily over his master, calling to him in that hollow and ghastly voice, like a hound baying.

I saw Yet drag himself up, eyes charged with fear, and make for the door to the lower regions. When he got there, he pulled an enormous bell-mouthed gun – I imagine it was a blunderbuss – from his belt and levelled it at the monster.

Instinctively, I threw myself down. The monster turned. He threw up one arm and gave a great cry as the gun went off.

Noise and smoke filled the room.

Yet went blundering down the stairs.

'You killed my master! Now you have wounded me!' cried the monster. With a bound, he was up and giving chase, hurling himself down the stairs. Cries from Yet as he fled.

The noise had its effect on Frankenstein. He groaned and stirred. I saw that he would be coming to in a minute. I dashed the remainder of the wine in his face to revive him, and ran up to the laboratory again.

There was going to be murder before the night was through, and I had to get clear.

I slammed the door shut behind me, but there was no bolt on the inner side. Not that I imagined that any bolt could keep out that terrible avenging creature!

The female still lay there, watery eyes staring at some remote distance from which she waited to be recalled. I crossed behind her, and seized a pair of steps, used to reach the higher shelves. I dragged the steps to the middle of the room, climbed them, swung myself up through the skylight by which the monster had entered.

Supernaturally strong though the monster was, I could not visualize its being able to scale the sheer outside wall of the tower. Therefore it had made itself a ladder. Had not Victor mentioned some such possibility?

It was freezingly cold and entirely dark on the roof, despite the snow everywhere.

Nervously, I moved forward, fumbling round the battlements until I came to a protruding wooden pole. Here was the ladder. Only the terror of being caught by the creature – I could all too clearly imagine myself being hurled from the roof – drove me to climb over into space and feel for the first rung of the ladder. But – there it was, and I began to go down as quickly as possible but with difficulty, for there was almost a metre between rungs.

At length I stood on the ground, up to my ankles in fresh-fallen snow.

First I pulled the great ladder away from the tower, sending it crashing back into the trees. Then I went round to the gate, to listen there, in an agony of apprehension.

Banging noises sounded from within. There was the clang of metal as a bar was withdrawn. A small door in the big gates was flung open. Yet emerged, staggering drunkenly and clutching his shoulder.

By now, my sight had adjusted to the dark. I was hidden behind a tree, but could see his dark barrel-shaped silhouette clearly enough. Behind him, something was fighting to get out of the door. It was the monster. Instinctively, I ducked back a tree or two. Yet stood in the clearing as if undecided. He ambled over to the nearest tree – happily some metres from where I stood hidden, and turned towards the tower.

Then I realized that he was wounded, and could not run; and that he carried a sword in his hand.

The monster still struggled to climb through a door too small for his immense frame. He wrenched at the stout panelling, roaring with fury. With a splintering noise, it fell beneath his pressure. He broke through, and was across the clearing that separated him from Yet in a twinkling.

Yet had time for one blow. Maybe it was a sabre he held. I saw a broad blade flash dimly, heard it strike the sleeve of the monster's greatcoat. A ferocious growl came from the monster. He gave Yet no time to strike again.

First he flung the man head-first into the snow. Then he

sprang savagely on top of him, and grappled him by the throat — as once he must have grappled with little William. And Yet could put up no more resistance than William.

In a moment, the monster rose, lurching slightly, and started to head back for the dark tower. Behind him, Yet lay lifeless in the snow.

21

'You have killed again!' cried Victor Frankenstein.

He stood in the shattered doorway, confronting his monster, a shadow among shadows. From where I stood, I could see only that sharp-cut face of his, blurred by dark and passion.

The monster stopped before him. 'Master, why do you misrepresent my every action? I attacked your servant only because I believed he had killed you. Your possessions and your servants are sacred to me, as well you know! Be propitious while I speak — hast thou not made me here thy substitute?'

'Cease to quote your Miltonic scriptures at me! You dare say thus, Fiend, and yet you threaten the life of my fiancée?'

To this the monster had nothing to say, but stood silent. They remained as they were; in some fashion they were communing, and I could sense from my vantage point the necessity that linked them. Perhaps the monster could never be dominated, yet Frankenstein, being human, could not resist the attempt.

'You remonstrate with me, you thing of evil, when your hands are still wet with the blood of my brother William. I know you brought about his death, whatever the court said on that score.'

Then the monster spoke in his desolate voice. 'You must abide by the verdict of the court, for you perforce come within human jurisdiction. It has no such claim on me, being without humanity. I say only this — that perplexed and troubled at my bad success, as was the Tempter, I struck at you through William. He to me was a limb of you, even as I am.'

'And that filthy deed you put on to another.'

At this, the monster gave a laugh like a whipped bloodhound. 'I ripped the locket from his sanguined throat and tucked it into the pocket of the maid where she slept. If she was hanged for that, so much for man's legal institutions!'

'For that piece of devilry you will be well repaid, never fear!'

The creature growled in its throat. Again they ran out of words. Victor remained in the shattered door. The nameless one waited outside, its outline blurred by the slow ascent of steam from its clothes. Lizards could not have been more still until the creature spoke again, this time with a note of pleading in its voice.

'Let me enter into the tower, my Creator, and let me see you bring life to the mate I know you have prepared, manlike but different sex, so lovely fair. And then – since you cannot find it in your heart to love me – we will go our separate ways, for ever and ever, never to meet more. You shall go where you will. I will dwell in the frigid lands with my bride, and no man shall ever set eyes on us again!'

Again silence.

Finally, Frankenstein said, 'Very well, so shall it be, since it cannot be otherwise. I will give life to the female. Then you must go and nevermore afflict my eyesight.'

The great creature fell on its knees in the snow. I saw it reach out its hand towards Frankenstein's boots.

'Master, I will feel only gratitude, that I swear! The thoughts that torment me I will forget. I am your slave. How I wish that but once before you banish me we might converse together on fragrant subjects! What a world you might open up to me ... yet all we ever speak of together is guilt and death, I know not why. The grave is never far from my meditations, Master, and when the boy died in my clutch – oh, you cannot understand, it was as Adam said, a sight of terror, foul and ugly to behold, horrid to think, how horrible to feel! Speak to me once in loving tones of better things.'

'Do not fawn! Get up! Stand away! You must come with me into the tower to accomplish this foul work, since Yet is slain – I need your aid stoking the boilers to keep the electricity at full voltage. Enter and be silent.'

Moaning, the creature rose, saying impulsively, 'When I found you just now, I feared you were killed also, Master.'

'Confound you, I was not killed but drugged. Maybe it would have been better for me otherwise! That interfering Bodenland was to blame. If you encounter him, Fiend, you may exercise your fiendishness on him without restraint!'

They were now moving inside. I followed to the door and heard the creature's rebuke by way of reply.

'The breaking of necks is no pleasure for me. I have my religious beliefs, unlike you inventors rare, unmindful of your Maker, though His spirit taught you! Besides, Bodenland expressed some gratitude to me – the only man ever to do so!'

'What religious system could ever light a light within your skull!' said Frankenstein contemptuously, leading the way upstairs, where a shaft of light indicated an open door into the machine room. They climbed through, and the door closed behind them.

For a while I stood by the shattered doorway, wondering what to do. Plenty of timber lay about the building. Maybe I could stack it up and set the place alight, so that they – and that terrible female they were now conspiring to bring to life – would perish in the flames, together with all Frankenstein's instruments and notes. But how could I get a fire going fast enough to catch them? For they would escape before the fire took hold.

The steam engine began to work faster overhead. Protected by the noise, which surely signified the most hideously active stoking the world had ever seen, I began to search about, even daring to light a flambeau, which was all this ground floor seemed to warrant in the way of illumination.

Plenty of wood and timber lay about, as well as skins of wine and various provisions. To one side stood the phaeton. Beyond that was a stable, with the horse standing there indifferently, uncaring what passed before its eyes as long as it had food. Pushing its head out of the way, I thrust the flambeau into its stall, to see if there might be kerosene or paraffin stored there, or at least a good stack of hay.

An even more welcome sight met my eyes.

There stood my automobile, the Felder, unharmed, almost unscratched!

Amazed, I went into the stable, closing the lower door behind me. The stable was located in the square building adjoining the base of the tower. I saw there was a large door here leading straight outside. My vehicle had been pushed through it.

One of the car doors hung open. I extinguished my torch and climbed in, switching on one of the overhead lights. Everything was in disorder, but I could not see that anything had been taken.

I found a sheet of paper, a certificate which formally handed the vehicle over to the Frankenstein family. It was signed by the Geneva Chief of Police. So Elizabeth had been careful to acquire the car as some compensation for her fiancé's supposed murder! But what had Victor made of it? He must have towed it here for further investigation. Had he understood it for what it was? Would that explain why he asked me so few questions, took my unlikely presence and knowledge so much for granted? How precious would this car be to him? What new developments in science would he be able to deduce from the features of my automobile and its contents?

Checking the firearms, I found the swivel-gun was intact; a Browning .380 automatic was also present, together with its box of shells. I flung the sporting pistol I had looted on to the back seat, relieved to think I would never have to defend myself with it.

It occurred to me that, only a generation before mine, automobiles had been fuelled by gasoline. Gasoline would have been ideal for a sudden blaze; the sealed nuclear drive was useless in that respect.

Having the car gave me other ideas. A fire would always be an easy thing from which a superhuman creature like the monster could escape. A hail of bullets was quite another matter.

Working as quietly as I could, pausing every now and again to listen, I opened the outer gate wide. This entailed shovelling away a considerable drift of snow. Then I attempted to push the vehicle into the open.

I got my shoulder to it and heaved. It would not budge.

After some exertion, I decided the track was too rutted for me to have a hope. Since I would have to start the engine some time in any case, it might be best to do so now, cloaked by the noise of the steam engine thudding somewhere overhead.

Praise be for the twenty-first century! The Felder started immediately, and I watched the revs climbing on the rev-counter until I began to roll forward into the open. What a feeling of power to be back at the wheel again!

Once I was outside, I left the engine running and ran back to close the gate. Then I manoeuvred the auto among the trees, until I set it – according to my estimation – in the perfect position, some way from the main gates of the tower, but having them in view even in the present dismal light. Then I raised the blister, and focused the swivel-gun.

All I had to do was squeeze the button when someone emerged from the tower. It was the best solution. The extra-ordinary stop-start conversation between Victor and his monster had convinced me of the latter's supreme dangerousness: given its malevolence, its lying and eloquent tongue was prob-ably as big a threat as its turn of speed.

Time passed. The hours slid slowly down the great entropy slope of the universe.

The snow ceased. A slender moon appeared.

My labouring minutes were occupied with fantasies of the most horrific kind. While the monster stoked, was Victor find-ing time to perform a facial operation on the female? Or was he ... Enough of that. I would have given a good deal to have the stalwart Lord Byron by me, armed with the handgun.

Although visibility improved with moonlight, I was not happy at the improvement. The car might now be noticed from the entrance to the tower, whereas I had set it in shadow. Although it might seem that the advantage was heavily enough with me, ensconced behind a swivel-gun, still there was that memory of improved musculature, of fantastic jumps and fast runs, of irascibility coupled with power. Just suppose that creature eluded my first stream of bullets and got to me before I could kill it ...

Chilly though I was, the supposition chilled me more. I jumped out of the car and began to collect up fallen pine branches with which to camouflage the vehicle.

While I was some metres away from it, the ruined door of the tower was flung wide and the monster emerged.

A fleeting recollection, as the dying are supposed to relive past episodes: recollection of my old sane ordered life now lost by two centuries, of my dear wife, my valued friends, even some of my esteemed enemies, and of my little grandchildren. I recalled how sane and healthy they were, and I contrasted them with the fiends with whom I had to deal in 1816!

Dropping the branches, I started what I feared would be a hopeless run back to the Felder. Foolishly, I had not even brought the automatic with me.

I reached the automobile. I scrambled in.

Only then did I turn to see what was happening, and how near my pursuer was.

22

Great flat-topped sheets of cloud were moving out of the frigid lands, intermittently obscuring the moon. The scene by the tower was rendered in untrustworthy washes of light.

Frankenstein's monster stood outside the shattered door. He was not looking at me at all. He stared back in to the dark from which he had emerged. I thought that one of his hands was extended. He took a pace back to the door.

There was a hesitancy in his manner which was entirely strange. Someone took his hand. A figure emerged from the doorway, a figure almost as gigantic as he. It staggered, and he caught its elbow. They stood together, heads almost touching.

He made her walk to and fro. I saw their breath on the frosty air. He was supporting her, an arm about her enormous waist. Her lumbering footsteps kicked up small flurries of snow.

She was weak from post-operative shock, and had to lean against the wall. Her face was turned upwards towards the night sky. Her mouth opened.

He left her, moving with that terrible needless alacrity back into the tower. From my hiding place, I strained to see her more clearly. Moonlight washed over her features, making of her eyes a perfect blank. It no longer looked like Justine. Another life occupied it.

The monster returned, bearing a goblet. He forced her to drink despite her protests. She drank, and he flung the glass down, standing back from her to see what she did.

She came uncertainly forward, step by step, feeling for her balance. She stood, arms extended but bent, and slowly moved her head from side to side. She turned with an automatic movement and began to walk, swaying from side to side at first, but gradually gaining a more regular rhythm.

He dashed about her, solicitous but irascible. At one stage, he joined her, pacing with her, beating time with one hand. Then he stood aside again, still conducting, urging her to move faster. She went to lean against the wall – he made a vehement negative gesture – she staggered forward again.

He began to run about in front of her, to turn, to perform grotesque dance movements that were not without some grace. She came to him hesitantly, and he took both her hands in his. Hesitantly, they began to trip from side to side, facing each other, he always encouraging her, like two lunatic children in a dance.

She had to rest. He supported her, staring up at the tower. She was holding her side and explaining something.

With a human gesture, he cupped his mouth with one hand and called upwards into the night.

'Frankenstein!'

As that great hollow voice sounded, dogs began barking in a nearby village, and were answered more distantly by wolves up in the hills.

No reply came from the tower.

After a rest, the pair began to dance again. Then he released her and ran about, as slowly as he could. She followed ponderously. Once she fell over, sprawling in the snow. He was upon her instantly, lifting her up with tender clumsy care, holding her scarred head against his cheek.

He urged her to run again. He cantered behind the tower. She followed. She was cautious at first, but her movements were coordinating rapidly. She found she could wave her arms as she ran. He stood back to watch in admiration, hands on tattered knees.

A strange mooing noise broke from them, which roused the dogs again. She was laughing!

Now she gestured to him to follow her. She set off round the tower, with him in playful pursuit. They were as sportive as a pair of shire horses. When she reappeared, her bald head gleaming dully, her arms were extended and she was making the mooing noise again. To keep her moving, he pretended to be unable to catch her.

As he ran, his hair streamed behind that helmet-skull like a plume.

Her actions were less clumsy now, her movements faster. She stopped suddenly. He clasped her about the waist, she pushed him away with a gesture that would have felled a man. There she stood, moving her arms, her wrists, her hands, like a Balinese dancer at practice. She was grotesquely dressed in what I took to be nothing more than the two sheets that had covered her on the bench, clumsily knotted about her vast frame; perhaps because of that, there was something poignant in those androgynous movements parodying grace.

Night brightened sharply, as if the moon had just disentangled itself from cloud. I looked up, startled to find how I had forgotten everything but the antics of these two monstrous beings.

Dual moons sailed in the sky.

One moon was the crescent that until now had claimed sole tenancy of the night. The other, an extended hand's span away from it, was almost full. They peered down on the world like two eyes, one half-closed.

The disintegration of space/time was still taking place! – only this thought came to me not in any orderly way but as a confused recollection of a passage in Shakespeare's *Julius Caesar*—

And graves have yawned and yielded up their dead;
Fierce fiery warriors fight upon the clouds ...
The heavens themselves blaze forth the death of princes.

Death was very much on my mind, yet I could not tear my attention away from the cavortings of those two inhuman beings. Almost as if they had been awaiting the signal of an extra moon, they now took their prancings into a more intense phase. They stayed much more closely together, weaving intricate patterns round each other.

Sometimes she stood still, providing a centre for the storm of his movement; sometimes the roles were reversed, and he stood tensely while she whirled about him. Then their mood would change, and they would languorously intertwine and writhe as if to the stately music of a sarabande. They were now deeply into their mating dance, oblivious to all that went on beyond the charmed circle of their courtship. Two moons in one sky were nothing to them.

Again a change of mood. The tempo grew wilder. They danced away from each other, they darted towards each other. Occasionally, one would flick snow at the other – although by now the snow was well trampled over a wide area. As their motions became faster, so they moved in wider and wider gyrations. They were nearing the auto now, plunging towards it, backing away, seeing nothing but each other. I was too hypnotized to move. My plan to use the swivel-gun was gone from my head.

When she came very near, I had a clear view of her face, turned brightly to the moonlight. There I read conflicting things. It was the intent face of female in rut – yet it was also the face of Justine, impersonal with death. If anything, *his* face was even more horrific, lacking as it did all but a travesty of humanity; despite his animation, it still most resembled a helmet, a metal helmet with visor down, roughly shaped to conform to the outlines of a human face. The helmet had a tight slit across it, representing a smile.

They joined hands, they twirled round and round and round. She broke away, uttering that mooing noise. She began to circle the tower again. Again he followed.

The wolves were howling closer at hand. Their discord provided accompaniment for the chase that now developed between the two beings. She darted round and round the tower, running fast but waving her hands. He kept close behind, not exerting himself. As the pace hotted up, panic entered her movements. She began to run in earnest, he to follow in earnest. I cannot say at what speed they moved, or how many times she circled the base of the tower, running as if her life depended on it. He was calling, making inarticulate noises, grunting and angry.

Finally, when his hand was on her shoulder, she half-turned, slapped his arm away, and made as if to burst inside the tower for sanctuary. He seized her in the doorway.

She screamed, a hoarse tenor noise, and fought. With one great heave of his hand, he ripped her flimsy garments from her.

I saw that her reluctance to be taken had been feigned, or part-feigned. For she stood before him naked and brazen, and began again a slow weaving movement of her limbs, without departing from where she stood. I could see the great livid weals of scars running across the small of her back and down her mighty thighs.

He remained in a half-crouch watching her, the smile of the helmet very narrow now. Then he sprang, bearing her down into the trampled snow only a few paces from Yet's body.

That narrow smile was pressed to the scars on Justine's throat. She half-rose at one point, but he bore her down again. She gave her tenor scream, and the wolves answered. A light uneasy wind licked through the bushes.

It was a brief and brutal mating.

Then they lay on the ground like two dead trees.

She rose first, searching out her sheets and knotting them indifferently about her torso. He got up. Gesturing that she was to follow him, he began to march along the path that led down the hill, and was quickly out of sight. She followed. In a moment, she too had disappeared.

I was alone, dry of mouth, sick at heart.

23

For a while, I paced up and down in the clearing, consumed by a mixture of emotions. Among them, I have to confess, was lust, reluctantly aroused by that unparalleled mating. A natural if unfortunate association of ideas made me think of Mary and wonder where she was, in this increasingly confused universe. Sanctity and obscenity lie close in the mind.

Along with my self-disgust went anger. For I had meant to slay the monster. There would have been no glory in it; it would just have been a brutal ambush, keeping myself as far out of danger as possible; but I had conceived it my duty to kill the creature – and his maker, too, for the same reason, that both represented a threat to mankind, perhaps even to the natural order. Had compunction stayed my hand, or mere curiosity?

I felt little pride in myself, and knew I would feel still less when I had finished with Victor Frankenstein. He was still on the scene.

Or could it be that his monsters had killed him after he had brought life to the female? No doubt that might have been their intention; certainly Victor had suspected as much. By remaining on his guard, he could have eluded them.

I had not seen him leave the tower; maybe he had slipped out by the back way. It was more likely that he would still be hiding in the tower, in which case I had to seek him out, which meant venturing back into those hateful rooms where machinery had pounded.

My argument with myself had brought me to a standstill in the snow.

The body of Yet sprawled not far away. Wolves lurked in the forest. I saw green eyes among the trees. But I had the automatic in my pocket, and was not afraid of them in the midst of so much that was more alarming.

Cupping my hand, I shouted at the tower, 'Frankenstein!'

Complete silence. I should have said that the throb of machines had died some while ago, during the early stages of the mating dance. I was about to call again, when there was a movement in the dark beyond the shattered door, and Victor emerged into the clearing.

'So you are still about, eh, Bodenland? Why don't you fall silent on your knees before me? I gather you witnessed what I have achieved! I have done something that no other man has done! The power over life and death now belongs to mankind: at last the wearying cycle of the generations has been broken and an entirely new epoch is inaugurated . . .'

He stood with his arms above his head, unconsciously apeing the stance of an old prophet.

'Come to your senses, man! You know you have merely succeeded in creating a pair of fiends that will multiply and add to man's already great miseries. What makes you think they have not left here in all haste for Geneva and your house, where Elizabeth lives?' It was a cruel idea to stab him with, and he immediately showed its effect.

'My creature swore to me – swore by the names of God and Milton! – that as soon as his mate was created he would flee with her to the frigid lands, never to return to the haunts of men. He swore that!'

'What is his oath worth? Haven't you created a patched thing without an immortal soul? How can it have a conscience?'

I drew my automatic, wondering if I could work myself up to kill him. He seized my other arm, pleadingly. 'No, don't shoot, don't be foolish! How can you slay *me*, who alone understands these fiends, when you spared the fiends themselves? Listen, I had no alternative but to galvanize the tissues of that female into life – you saw how he threatened me. But there is a sure way how we can rid the world of them both. Let me create a *third* creature—'

'You're crazy!' Dawn was filtering in now. I could see the frenzy of enthusiasm in his face. A wind stirred.

'Yes, a third! Another male! Already I have many of the parts. Another male would seek out my first creation in the frigid lands. Jealousy would do the rest ... They would fight over the female and kill each other ... Put away your pistol, Bodenland, I beg – I beg of you! Look, come inside, come upstairs, let me explain, let me show you my future plans – you are civilized ...'

He moved into the tower. My will paralysed, I followed, still holding the automatic before me. There was a roaring in my ears, a desperate sickness overcoming me; my indecision thundered through me like waves.

I was following him up the stairs again, listening to his voice, which babbled on, wavering between sense and nonsense, as he too was seized by fear and fever. The figure of death – all its factors of cruelty, sadness, and hate – was compounded between us. Sickly colours were in the air, whirring about us like moiré patterns.

'. . . no purpose in life on this globe – only the endless begetting and dying, too monstrous to be called Purpose – just a phantasmagoria of flesh and flesh remade, of vegetation intervening – humans are just turnips, ploughed back at the end of the winter – the soil, the air, that linkage – like Shelley's west wind – the leaves could be us – you know, you understand me, Bodenland, "like ghosts from an enchanter fleeing, yellow and black and pale and hectic red, pestilence-stricken multitudes . . ." Did you ever think it might be life that was the pestilence, the accident of consciousness between the eternal chemistry working in the veins of earth and air? So you can't – you mustn't kill me, for a purpose must be found, invented if necessary, a human purpose, *human*, putting *us* in control, fighting the *itness* of the great wheeling world, Bodenland. You see, Bodenland? You're – you're an intellectual like me, I know it – I can tell – personalities must not enter into it, *please* – we have to be above the old considerations, be ruthless, as ruthless as the natural processes governing us. It stands to reason. Look—'

We had mounted somehow to his living-room, transfigured by crisis like creatures in a Fuseli canvas. I was still pointing the automatic at him. He stumbled towards a desk as he was talking, opened a drawer, bent, began to pull something from it—

I fired from close range.

He looked up at me. His face was transformed in some terrible way I could not explain – it no longer looked like his face. He brought a child's skull out into the light, placed it shakingly on the desk-top.

In a sepulchral and choked voice, he said, 'Henry will make a suitable husband for—'

A ragged cough broke through his speech. Blood spurted from his mouth. He put a hand to his chest. I made a move forward.

'A husband for—'

Again the blood.

'Victor—' I said.

His eyes closed. He was a small, frail man, young. He collapsed delicately, sinking rather than falling to the floor. His head went against the carpet with a gesture of weariness. Another choking cough, and his legs kicked.

Perched on an ancient folio, the baby's skull stared at me. Outside, the wolves were howling still.

24

When I let the horse go free and set fire to the tower of Frankenstein, it was as much to burn out my crime as to have an end to Frankenstein's notes and researches. Yet one of his notebooks I did keep; it was a diary of his progress, and I preserved it in case I ever managed to return to my own time.

Well, we will say it like that. But my original personality had now almost entirely dissolved, and the limbo I was in seemed to me the only time I knew. I did what I did.

Leaving a great column of smoke behind me, I climbed into my automobile and drove to see if the Villa Diodati and the Campagne Chapuis were still in existence on this plane.

They were not. The frigid lands began no more than a stone's throw from where Mary's door had stood. It will seem odd to say I was relieved; but there was relief in the discovery, for I felt myself too soiled to approach her again. There had been periods in my earlier life when the apocalyptic nature of some event – say a severe personal humiliation – had caused me to return ever and again to it, obsessively, in memory; not just to recall it, but to *be* there again, in an eternal return such as Ouspenski postulates, as if some pungently strong emotion could cause time to close back on itself like a fan. But those occasions were nothing to the obsessive return in the toils of which I was now involved. I could not rid myself of Victor's death, or of the mating dance. The two happened simultaneously, were one linked event, one in violence, one in the annihilation of personality, one in their intolerable disintegrative charge.

Between the blinding voltages of these returns, I attempted to make my brain think. At least the graven image of reality had been destroyed for me, so that I no longer had difficulty in apprehending Frankenstein and his monsters, Byron, Mary Shelley, and the world of 2020 as contiguous. What I had done – so it seemed – was wreck the *fatalism* of coming events. If Mary Shelley's novel could be regarded as a possible future, then I had now rendered it impossible by killing Victor.

But Victor was not real. Or rather, in the twenty-first century from which I came (there might be others from which I had not come), he existed only as a fictitious, or, at best, legendary character; whereas Mary Shelley was an historical figure whose remains and portraits could be dwelt on.

In that world, Victor had not reached the point of emerging from possibility to probability. But I had come to an 1816 (and there might be countless other 1816s of which I knew nothing) in which he shared – and his monster shared – an equal reality with Mary and Byron and the rest.

Such thought opened dizzy vistas of complexity. Possibility and time levels seemed as fluid as the clouds which meet and merge eternally in northern skies, forever changing shape and altitude. Yet even the clouds are subject to immutable laws. In the flux of time, there would always be immutable laws. Would character be a constant? I had regarded character as something so evanescent, so malleable; not that I saw a fatalism there, in Mary's melancholy, in Victor's anxious scientific drive, in my own curiosity. These were permanent factors, though they might be reinforced by accidental events, the drowning of Shelley, let us say, or a basic lack of sympathy in Elizabeth.

Somewhere, there might be a 2020 in which I existed merely as a character in a novel about Frankenstein and Mary.

I had altered no future, no past, I had merely diffused myself over a number of cloud-patch times.

There was no future, no past. Only the cloud-sky of infinite present states.

Man was prevented from realizing this truth by the limitations of his consciousness. Consciousness had never evolved as an instrument designed to discover truth; it was a tool to hunt down a mate, the next meal.

If I came anywhere near to the truth now, it was only because my consciousness was slipping towards the extreme brink of disintegration.

All this reasoning – if it was that – might in itself be illusion, product of stress, or product merely of the timeslips. Space/time went on in my skull, just as in the rest of the universe!

I fell into a swooning sleep, drooped over the steering column.

When I woke, Victor was still with me, dying all over again, my hand reaching out as if to save him, as if in ridiculous apology.

Murder! I dared not think of God.

Well, I will try to say no more of this.

Frankenstein had gone. One thing remained for me. I had now to take on his role of monster-killer. Imperfectly though I recalled Mary's novel, I knew that her Frankenstein had embarked on a pursuit of his creature which had taken them both into those gloomy and ice-bound regions which held so strong a lure for the Romantic imagination.

For two days I drove along the fringes of the frigid lands which followed roughly the shores of the old lake, trying to pick up a trace of the two monsters. Wild and awful though I was, no human being questioned my appearance now. Their lives had been utterly disrupted. Their crops were ruined, their livelihood on the lake had vanished, and the winter promised starvation for all of them.

Extreme though the times were, the two monsters would have remained sufficiently remarkable, prodigies in a time of prodigies.

Towards sunset on the second day, I happened on a hamlet where a small child had been attacked by wolves in her father's back garden only the evening before.

There was a hostelry called the Silver Stag at which I made my inquiries. The owner said that his stable had been broken into the previous night, after he had gone to bed. He heard his dogs howling in the yard, had lit a lantern and gone down to see what was happening. An enormous man – a foreigner, he suspected – had come rushing from the stable, dragging the two best horses with him. After him came another great foreigner, pulling the donkey. He had tried to intervene and had been swept out of the way. He called to his neighbours for help. By the time they arrived, the two enormous thieves had gone, riding down the road with the innkeeper's dog, a German shepherd, still snapping at their heels. He took me and showed me how brutally the lock on the stable had been broken, and the adjacent timber shattered. I had seen such damage, such superfluous strength, before.

Close to starvation though the hamlet was, the lure of profit was still working. I paid dearly for some dried wurst and drove away in the direction the innkeeper indicated.

Once into the frigid lands, I paused to sleep and bring this account up to date. On the morrow, I would begin the pursuit.

25

Even before the time-broken landscape met my gaze next morning, Victor Frankenstein was there before my eyes as usual, falling as usual behind the old desk, unable as usual to speak Elizabeth's name for blood.

I climbed out of the car, performed my natural functions, rinsed my face in an icy stream. Nothing could refresh my soul; I was a Jonas Chuzzlewit, a Raskolnikov. I had lied, cheated, committed adultery, looted, thieved, and ultimately murdered; henceforth my only fit company was the two brutes who journeyed somewhere ahead of me, my only fit surroundings the frigid hinterlands of hell which I now entered. I had taken over Victor's role. Henceforth, there was only the hunt to the death.

Of the first part of that journey, I shall tell briefly.

The country over which I travelled reminded me of the tundra I had seen in parts of Alaska and the Canadian North-West. It was all but featureless, apart from an occasional lonely pine or birch tree. The surface consisted of uneven tussocks of rough grass and little else. The ground was generally marshy, with frequent pools lying amid the grass, from which I guessed that permafrost had formed underground, preventing the water from draining away.

Nor was the sun of sufficient power to draw up the surface moisture. I was in a land where sunshine had little effect.

It would be hard to say that there were tracks in this wilderness. Yet there were indications that men or animals travelled here, and an occasional wooden post had been raised, presumably as a marker. Now and again, a trail emerged.

Although my progress was slow, I knew that the quarry I sought could scarcely move at a faster rate. The going was quite as bad for horses as for automobiles.

Day followed day. Nothing can be said of them.

Then came the day when the nature of the land altered slightly. As I moved slowly forward, I saw the change ahead. It was marked by the land becoming rougher, the clumps of grass coarser and more upstanding, and the dark dull pools more frequent. More bushes stood out.

It was not impossible that another timeslip had been at work here, amalgamating two similar territories which had formerly lain many thousands of miles and maybe many thousands of centuries apart.

A slight incline marked the division between the territories. Here I found a distinct trail, branching two ways. I drove to the top of the incline, stopped, and climbed out to look about me, uncertain whether to take the left track or the right, although imbued with such fatalism that I almost believed I should strike the correct one whatever I did. But something had not been content to leave matters so to chance.

On the left hand track lay the body of an animal. I went across to it and saw it was the carcass of a fine German sheepdog. Its skull had been shattered by a blow. Its muzzle pointed along the trail.

Day followed day as I continued the journey. They were without distinction or differentiation. Not only was the weather icily still; the days themselves were without sunset, for the sun no longer sank below the land. Along the northern horizon, night travelled, its stain remaining there even at noon; but so high was the latitude – or so I had to presume – that the solar orb was never extinguished. Nor did it ever manage to rise far towards zenith. Instead, it undulated round the dismal horizon, never more than a few degrees above its rim. I was in a land where the dews and mists of protracted dawn merged indistinguishably with the damps and veiled splendours of a long-drawn-out sunset.

A mournful beauty infiltrated this period, in which the only persistent qualities were the most amorphous. Banks of mist, towers of cloud, layers of silvery fog, nondescript pools which reflected the curtained sky – these were the durable features of that place. Amid such a phantasmal landscape, small wonder if I saw phantoms: Victor forever clutching at his coat and falling behind the desk with a last dull glance towards me, the monster steaming as it leapt forward. But of living things there was none.

I am almost reluctant to say that change came. Yet it is ultimately the one permanent thing until the death of the universe.

That ineluctable change wrote itself on the envelope of colour and moisture around me so gradually, so tentatively, that it was many hours before I came to accept that there were objects ahead of me, materializing in the veils of mist.

At first they seemed to be merely the tops of tall conifers.

Then I believed that they were masts of ancient sailing ships, lying becalmed on an ocean somewhere within reach.

Then I saw that they were spires of old churches, old cathedrals, old towns, ancient cities.

It was of more immediate concern that I now came on a definite track. Although it was less than a sandy lane, frequently punctuated by pools of water, it gave the landscape purpose, and nothing interested me but purpose; I had become machine-like.

The track – soon it was marked enough to warrant being called a road – ran straight towards the shrouded horizon without touching on any of the old towns. Never did I see the base of one of those towns or cathedrals. Always, their spires floated on the beds of mist which blanketed the land. I recalled the paintings of a German Romantic artist, Caspar David Friedrich, with his embodiments of all that was gloomy and meagre about nature in the north. I could imagine myself in the still world of his art.

The towns I passed distantly held no attraction for me, their crumbling roofs, their Gothic spires, no promise. Other matters possessed me.

Nevertheless, fatigue still played a role in my world. It came to me that my hands were numb from clutching the steering wheel, that my body had stiffened almost immoveably, and that I no longer recollected who I was or had been. I was simply a travelling item, wheeled and inexhaustibly propelled. I had not slept for many days – certainly a week, possibly longer.

I turned down a side-track, striking at random for one of the towns.

Through the mists was the apparition of an ecclesiastical ruin, its gaunt buttresses palely washed in.

I pursued it, and came at last to the mouldering remains of a large abbey. Many stones and arches stood yet, while the entire west wall – its fine triple window a gaping hole – was almost intact, although crowned in ivy and similar parasitic vegetation.

On leaving the car, I saw an old fallen signpost, its arms pointing to places called Greifswald and Peenemünde. Then I realized it was one of a vast pile of decaying signs, all indicating various towns, and left here to rot indifferently. Perhaps the very destinations were no more.

In the shell of the once-noble building, a much humbler dwelling stood, looking for protection and support from the great wall which towered above it. I went towards it through thistle-patches with something like an echo of hope stirring in me, thinking I saw a light burn dimly in one window; it was only the eternal illusory sunset, reflected by glass. I found that the dwelling was deserted, itself a ruin, its walls crumbling, its thatch tumbling down about its upper windows. It seemed I was no longer intended for human company.

The house was tumbledown, and had been occupied by transients before. I did not care. Stiff and weary as I was, I lowered myself down on a couch to sleep, unmindful of how many mortals had done the same before me.

26

During that night without darkness, a wind sprang up, causing windows, shutters and doors to creak. The noises may have accounted for the nature of the visions which besieged me, crowding into a brain long deprived of its dreaming times.

Dear Mary was with me again. We were never able even to touch, but at least she was with me. Sometimes she was young and beautiful, and walked in the States with me, leading a sheltered life and meeting few people. Or she was a best-selling novelist, going everywhere, speaking to large gatherings, visiting the premieres of the films made from her novels. Sometimes she was with Shelley.

Sometimes she and I were utterly taken up with a search for Shelley. He was missing, and we moved through the countryside seeking for him. Her little face, looking upwards at mine, was pathetic – and not a face at all, I realized, but merely a limp hand, lying in snow. We were hastening along a boulder-strewn shore, searching for Shelley's boat. We were in the boat, staring down into limpid water. We were in the water, venturing into submarine caves. We were in a cavern, watching leaves blow before us. 'Those are the leaves of the Sybil,' said Mary. Once she was with her mother, a radiantly beautiful woman who smiled mysteriously as she climbed into a railway carriage.

I was with Shelley and Mary in the subordinate role of gardener. They were old now, although I had not aged. Mary was small and frail; she wore a bonnet. Shelley was bent but still amazingly quick in his movements. He had a long beard. He was a cabinet minister. He was my father. He was inventing a plant that would produce sirloin steak. He spoke with the sound of mandolins. He picked Mary up and tucked her into his pocket. He announced publicly that he was going to take over Greece in a week's time. He sat on a mossy stone and wept, refusing to be comforted. I offered him a bowl of something, but a raven ate it, whatever it was. He flew a kite and climbed swiftly up its string.

Byron was there. He had grown fat and wore a cocked hat.

'Nothing is against nature,' he told me, laughing, by way of explanation.

In my dream, I was glad to see Byron. I was asking him to be reasonable about some matter. He was busy being reasonable about something else entirely.

He opened a green door, and in came Mary and Shelley, eating oranges in rather a disgusting way. Shelley showed me a photograph of himself in which he looked skinny. Mary was old again. She introduced me to a young poet friend whose name was Thomas Hardy. He was doing something with some bricks, and told me he had admired the works of Darwin ever since he was a child. I asked him if he did not mean to name another poet. He smiled and said that Mary would understand better because she had been officially presented with – I forget what, something absurd, the Pomeranian flag . . .

So far, the dreams were flashes of trivial nonsense. I need not recall more. Then they took on a more sombre tone. An old friend escorted me to an enormous pile of rubbish. A woman was sitting in the sunset, cradling a baby. She was enormous. Her clothes appeared to be smoking. She wore a black hat.

The child kept up a squealing cry which its mother seemed not to notice. My friend was explaining that the cry was a certain voice-print of brain damage in the infant. He gave an exact name to the kind of damage, which I failed to hear. I was actively searching through the rubbish.

I found there were many infants in the great heap, all with wakeful eyes. Many had huge malignant pouchy foreheads coming almost to their noses. Maybe they were foetuses; in any case, I appeared to anticipate finding them there.

They were crying. So was Mina. She had changed. Something had wounded her. I thought her hair was on fire. A pig ran past, although we were in a crowded room. A man she knew was pulling a piano apart.

The noise of crying mingled with the sound of wind.

When I roused at last, it was some relief to find myself in that dismal house in the ruins and to some extent at least the master of my waking fate; although, as the nonsense in my brain sank back into its container, out stalked the image of Victor again, his face like a medallion, staggering, falling.

Or sometimes not falling. He was coming back to life. It

might be a sign that I was recovering from the first guilt of murder. He no longer invariably collapsed when I shot him.

Choked and digusted, I went back to the car and the endless pursuit.

The wind had blown the mists away. I saw herds of wild ponies on either side. The most striking feature of the landscape newly revealed was a line of mountains, not too far distant. Their peaks strutted above the forsaken cities, capped with snow and slow smouldering cloud. And my road led that way.

Since the way was clear, I accelerated, driving as fast as possible all that day, and the next, and the one after that. As I drew nearer the mountains, and they rose in my vision, the sun began setting regularly behind them; or rather, it would give a more accurate picture to say that, during the hours between sunset and sunrise, the mountains cast a great ragged shadow which swung round and outwards from their base, further and further, until it engulfed my tiny speeding vehicle.

Once I turned to look back in the direction I had come. The cities were still just visible. They all huddled together at one point on the plain – or so it appeared. They remained in sunlight.

At last the road began to climb. No longer did it run straight forward. It turned and coiled in order to find its way among the foothills.

There came a point when the plain had fallen some thousands of feet below and behind me. Here was a plateau and again a division of the road. A winding path lay to the left, a straight one – looking as if it might easily run downhill – leading to the right. By the left fork lay a length of muddy and blood-stained bandage. I turned that way and found myself, a day or two later, driving in valleys among snow-capped peaks.

The sense of repetition that then afflicted me will be familiar to anyone who has driven in mountainous country. The road winds and winds to reach one end of a giant recession into the mountains; then it winds in an opposite direction to reach a point but a short distance from the first as the crow flies. Then the same procedure must be repeated at the next re-entrant ... Now this process had to be repeated a hundred times, two hundred, three ...

Occasionally, my tired brain assured me it saw Victor running screaming before the vehicle, a hole in his lungs and blood at his throat.

I reached the snowline. Nothing grew here, nothing lived.

Still I drove, thinking my quarry must be near. Surely they could not have rivalled my swiftness over the plain!

I climbed towards a great pass.

Beyond were glaciers, snow, huge boulders, a broken line of further peaks. Despite the heating in the Felder, my bones were aware of an intense cold outside.

The walls of the pass were high eroded cliffs. The road ran under one cliff. To the other side was the first fan-shaped outcrop of a glacier. The glacier became larger as I drove along by its side, so that the road narrowed, trapped between cliff and glacier. Soon it was squeezed almost to nothing, so that I was forced to stop. There was no way to go further. My path was barred by the debris from the glacier.

Although I knew I had to get up the pass, there was nothing for it but to back away. I returned to the point where a moraine of stones and boulders marked the forward edge of the glacier.

At one spot, a way had been cleared among the stones. Something was lying there. Despite the cold, I climbed out to look. The bloodied leg of a horse, apparently wrenched from its socket, lay with its hoof pointing up into the heart of the glacier.

There was nothing for it but to accept this horrid invitation. I drove the vehicle forward on to the ice.

Travelling with caution, I soon discovered that the surface of ice provided no bad road. It was almost free of debris. Possibly it would be more correct to speak of my being on an ice stream rather than a glacier proper; but I am no expert in such matters. All I can say is that it looked increasingly as if I were in some part of Greenland.

The surface had a ripple pattern, rather like barred sand on a shore where the tide had gone out, which gave the tyres something to grip on.

I had increased speed when a crevasse appeared ahead. Braking immediately, I slowed the engine and threw it into reverse. But the automobile went into a skid, and its front wheels slipped over into the gulf.

I had to climb out. The crevasse was not deep, and not a metre wide. Yet I was securely trapped. I could fit an attachment to the vehicle's nuclear plant which would melt the ice. Or I could try to jack up the front axle. But neither expedient held any guarantee that the Felder would be freed.

Straightening, I looked about helplessly. What a wilderness of rock and ice! Far, far behind and below me, I could catch a glimpse of the plain between two crags. It was marked by little more than a blue-green line. How greatly I had ventured beyond all human contact!

Staring up the ice, in the direction I was planning to go, I saw a familiar figure. Pallid face, black coat, hand at throat as he moved dying over the ice. Victor, eternally returning.

He was calling to me, voice echoing hollowly over the unsympathetic surfaces about us.

I hid my eyes in the palms of my hands, but the voice still called. I looked again.

Two figures were up there, monstrous in outline, partly cancelled by the black-lit clouds that came boiling up from behind them and the peaks in the background. They were waving their clumsy arms above their heads to attract my attention. I could make out that they had with them a string of horses, some with packs on their backs. These were presumably a few of the wild horses I had observed on the plain.

For a moment, I was too much taken aback by their waving to make any gesture in return. Yet I was glad to see them there. They spoke my language. They were living things, or replicas thereof. Belatedly, it occurred to me that my mission was to kill them; by then, I had acknowledged their presence by waving.

Climbing back into the front seat, I raised the blister in the roof and brought up the muzzle of the swivel gun. If I killed them now, I could take over their horses and make my way back to human society. But with the auto so down on the front axle the firing angle was bad. I squinted at them through the telescopic sights and already they were half lost among shattered stones. Evidently satisfied that they had attracted my attention, they were moving on. As much for my own satisfaction as their dismay, I sent half-a-dozen rounds whining over their heads.

They disappeared. Only a pair of black horses remained to be seen. Laying my cheek against the gun, I stared up there where the world seemed to end, too blank of mind to wonder about my predicament. Only gradually did it dawn on me that, though the immense figures had gone with their train, the two horses remained tethered where they were. My quarry had left me a means of following them, of continuing the chase.

27

I attempted to hitch the two horses to the front axle and pull the vehicle out of the crevasse; but it would not budge, or moved only to fall back again. So I had to abandon it.

All I took from it were the remains of my food and water, this tape-memory, my sleeping bag, a stove from the camp-locker (last used on a picnic with Poll and Tony, many worlds ago), and the swivel-gun, which I unbolted from its frame. With the swivel-gun went several magazines of ammunition.

This equipment I loaded on to the smaller of the two horses. I dressed myself in as many clothes as I could, and mounted the other horse. We began to pick our way slowly up the glacier, which now became littered with detritus. The Felder was lost behind us; I left it with less regret than I had parted from my watch.

Night fell. Cold streams of air, evenly flowing, breathed on us. Overhead were stars; neither moon was in sight. I looked upwards to identify familiar constellations. Never had so many stars blazed forth — never so unrecognizably. I had been an amateur astronomer; the night sky was no stranger to me; yet I was puzzled. There seemed to be a Pole Star where it should be, and the constellation of Ursa Major, yet with additional stars scattered across it. Yet was not that also Ursa Major and the stars over *there*, lower down the sky and some degrees away, half-concealed by a shoulder of mountain? We picked our way forward so that more stars came into view . . .

Yes, I travelled in a dual universe. The rupture of space/time was spreading in a chain reaction. Who knew what galaxies might exist tomorrow night?

It was absurd to imagine that this damage would be allowed to go on. Already, back in the time from which I came, scientists would be working on the problem, producing some daring solution to it which would successfully put a patch on the damage done. As I intended to put a patch on the damage Victor Frankenstein had done.

Then I reflected that these thoughts could hardly be mine. At first, the jettisoning of my vehicle, like the earlier selling of my watch, had been meaningful to me. Now I was thinking like Victor himself. Tiredness was again invading my mind, conjuring up some of the shadows I had had to battle with back in the ruined cottage.

Rather than rest, I climbed off my horse and led the two beasts forward, determined to stay on my feet for the rest of the night.

But the night seemed to go on forever. Possibly winter had now come, and the sun had slipped below the horizon. It was still dark – or at least not light – when finally I reached the end of my climb and the glacier became level.

Sleep and its delusions had infiltrated my mind. Now I was completely awake again.

A great plateau stretched before me, its limits hidden. It was not entirely flat, exhibiting here and there broad depressions or swells, rather like a calm but frozen sea. Only later did I realize that it was almost that. The plateau was formed of ice, a tremendous weight of ice which completely covered the great mountains below, although a few peaks broke the surface here and there in the form of nunataks. Over this great icefield, the nunataks formed the only landmarks, with one staggering exception.

Far away across the icefield was a mighty building.

I halted the animals.

From where I stood, it was hard to grasp the size of that distant structure. It appeared to be round and to consist of little more than an immense outer wall. It was certainly inhabited. From within the walls came a glow of light – almost an atmosphere of light, reddish in colour, and punctuated by intenser beams of brightness moving within the central cloud.

Elsewhere, dull depression reigned. Yet this was no bastion of light. For all its brightness, it too – I attempt no paradox – radiated drabness.

My speculation was that this was the last refuge of humanity. The place was so remote that I could only believe the timeslips to have delivered me at a point many centuries – maybe many thousands or even millions of centuries – into futurity. So that I might be witnessing the last outpost of mankind after the sun had died, when the universe itself was far gone towards the equipoise of its death. I looked at my two mounts, their eyes reflecting the distant glow. They waited indifferently. At least I could rejoin my own kind, however unpropitious the circumstances.

As I moved forward at a better pace, it occurred to me to wonder why the enemy should have led me here to a refuge, rather than onward to destruction. Could it be that they also were intending to enter this place? Or were they waiting somewhere to tear me apart before I reached shelter?

Clouds were boiling across the sky, obscuring the maze of constellations and bringing snow. The blaze from the city (I will call it that for cities have taken many forms in history) was reflected on the clouds. Everything appeared to be getting brighter. It was almost as if the city housed a number of active volcanoes. Sparks were now flying above the ramparts, sending bouquets of multi-coloured flame from one end to the other. The searchlight effect was also more powerful. It was as if some kind of celebration was taking place.

Drawing nearer, I could make out that there were gates set in the immense outer walls. And I saw towers within, obscured rather than illuminated by the flickering blaze. It was difficult to gauge size. I suspected they were enormous buildings. Certainly they were imposing; but dystopian visions of buildings come so close to celestial visions that I hardly knew whether the sight of them filled me with comfort or foreboding.

The horses shook their heads and whinnied. I went cautiously, for we were approaching a nunatak, and I feared ambush. I brought up my automatic in a gloved hand.

By now, I appreciated that we rode over thick ice. Shards of it, and shattered slate and stone, fringed the nunatak like a bleak shore. It was possible that this low and scoured dune marked the top of some once-proud mountain, now all but lost under the ice sheet. In its shelter stood a line of four horses, bridled and hobbled. My quarry had abandoned them, and must be on foot.

There was no sign of the two monsters.

I unloaded the swivel-gun and carried it to the top of the nunatak, sheltering it from the falling snow with my canvas packs. To protect myself from the cold to some extent, I climbed into my sleeping bag before lying down. Then I peered through the telescopic sights and endeavoured to find trace of my quarry.

There they were! Their figures were difficult to discern against the great dark walls ahead. But their outlines were fitfully picked out by the red light, as the moon first shows itself in crescent form. They had reached the city and were about to go in.

A new suspicion came coldly upon me. I had no guarantee that this city was built by human hands. To what human city would these two outcasts go in such a manner? This was a city that would welcome them – that indeed might be heralding them by a tremendous extravagance of light. This was their sort of city. This was a city built and occupied by their own kind. The future might be theirs and not ours.

Speculation. Confirmation or otherwise must come later.

I jammed a magazine into the breach of the gun. Its code told me that one bullet in five was tracer. A gate was opening in the distant city. From beyond it, light poured over the two enormous figures. I began firing as they started to enter.

A bright line of fire plunged across the intervening space. I saw the first bullets strike, and kept on firing, mouth tight, eye jammed to the sight. One of the figures – the woman – seemed to blaze. She spun about. Her arms jerked up in anger. More tracer poured into her. She appeared to break apart as she fell.

He – he also was hit! But he ran away from the light, so that I no longer had a silhouette as target. I had lost him. Then the sight found him again! He was coming! Making full use of that terrible deadly speed, he was racing across the ice towards me, arms and legs plunging in a speed no human could rival.

There was a glimpse of that cruel grinning helmet of a face as I wrenched the barrel round for better aim. It stuck.

Cursing, I looked down. One side of my sleeping-bag had caught in the gun's track. It was a moment's work to tear it loose, but in that moment he was nearly up to me.

With a strength almost beyond myself, I raised the gun and fired it from my hip. The tracer caught him as he charged up the slope.

Fire burned at his chest. A great bellow of fury broke from him. He fell backwards, tearing at his burning clothes.

Shooting off just one burst of tracer had almost broken my body in two. I had to drop the swivel-gun, collapsing to my knees as I did so.

But fear of the monster drove me on. I saw him roll smoking down the slope of the nunatak, to lie face down among rock and ice shards, flames licking at his foul greatcoat. The horses, in wild dismay, broke their tethers and went galloping away across the plains of ice.

Clutching my automatic, I went slowly down to where the great figure lay. It stirred now, turned over, drew itself into a sitting position. Its face was black. Smoke obscured it.

Even in ruin, the monster still exerted that tremendous paralysis of fascination which had deflected my purpose before. I levelled the gun at him, but did not fire – not even when I saw him gather himself to spring to his feet.

He spoke. 'In trying to destroy what you cannot understand, you destroy yourself! Only that lack of understanding makes you see a great divide between our natures. When you hate and fear me, you believe it is because of our differences. Oh, no, Bodenland! – It is because of our similarities that you bring such detestation to bear upon me!'

He could not rise. A hollow cough burst from him, and a change took place in that abstract helmet which was his face. The sutures of Frankenstein's surgery parted, ancient cicatrices opened at every contour; the whole countenance cracked, and I saw slow blood ooze in the apertures. He put a hand up – not to his cheeks, but to his chest, where the greater pain was.

'We are of different universes!' I said to him. 'I am a natural creature, you are a – a horror, unalive! I was born, you were made—'

'Our universe is the same universe, where pain and retribution rule.' His words were thick and slow. 'Our deaths are both a quenching out. As for our births – when I first opened my eyes, I knew I existed – as did you. But who I was, or where, or from what cause, I knew not – no more did you! As for those intervals between birth and destruction, my intentions, however warped, are more lucid to me than yours to you, as I suspect. You know not compassion—'

A spasm of pain possessed him, so that he could not speak.

Again I nerved myself to fire; a rocket flashed into the sky and burst overhead, deflecting me from my purpose. It opened into three great clusters of flame which hung there, silent, before fading. A signal, perhaps; to whom or what I knew not.

Before the lurid light went out, the monster at my feet said, 'This I will tell you, and through you all men, if you are deemed fit to rejoin your kind: that my death will weigh more heavily upon you than my life. No fury I might possess could be a match for yours. Moreoever, though you seek to bury me, yet will you continuously resurrect me! Once I am unbound, I am unbounded!'

On the word 'resurrect', delivered with ferocity, the fallen creature heaved himself to his feet and stood confronting me, fire still creeping at his chest and throat. Although he was below me on the slope, he dominated me.

I fired three times, aiming into that voluminous greatcoat. On the third shot, he went down on to one knee and gave a loud cry, clutching his head. When he looked up again, one side of his face, it appeared to me, had fallen away.

'There will be no more of you!' I said. Sudden triumph and calm filled me.

The creature was gone beyond my influence. He saw me no more. But he spoke again before he died.

'They thought me gone, for I that day was absent, as befell, bound on a voyage uncouth and obscure, far on excursion towards the gates of hell, where . . .'

A last attempt to rise, then he lost balance and fell forward, lying face down, one arm twisted out sideways with a clumsy gesture, palm upwards. I left him amid ice and thin smoke, to climb back up the nunatak. The monster was finished, and my quest.

Trembling, I set the swivel-gun to rights. If other attackers came for me, they should meet the same reception as the monster before I met my Maker. Or there might be men in the city; I must assume nothing more until more was known. Certainly they were aware of my presence. Since the rocket died overhead, the lights were being extinguished behind the great ramparts, the activity was ending, the displays were being put away. They would know where I was, and what I had done.

So I would wait here until someone or something came for me, biding my time in darkness and distance.